I0687597

From Strangers to Lovers

by

Tiffani Lynn

Betrayal to Bliss Book Two

This is a work of fiction. Names, characters, places, and incidents are either the product of the author's imagination or are used fictitiously, and any resemblance to actual persons living or dead, business establishments, events, or locales, is entirely coincidental.

From Strangers to Lovers

COPYRIGHT © 2017 by Tiffani Lynn

All rights reserved. No part of this book may be used or reproduced in any manner whatsoever without written permission of the author or The Wild Rose Press, Inc. except in the case of brief quotations embodied in critical articles or reviews.

Contact Information: info@thewildrosepress.com

Cover Art by *Diana Carlile*

The Wild Rose Press, Inc.
PO Box 708
Adams Basin, NY 14410-0708

Visit us at www.thewilderroses.com

Publishing History
First Scarlet Rose Edition, 2017
Print ISBN 978-1-5092-1396-2
Digital ISBN 978-1-5092-1397-9

Published in the United States of America

**Hope after heartbreak, love after loss,
and a future she never dreamed possible…**

"If you don't feel anything for me then just say it. If you do, stop wasting our time and let nature takes its course. What's it going to be, Jill?"

"I want you. I want there to be an us, but it's not the right thing. You've got to know that. I'm your brother's ex, the woman he cheated with. That's messed up, Johnny. It'll never be okay for us to be together."

His eyes and face lower to look at the asphalt. He shakes his head, and I'm wondering what he'll say next. He doesn't speak; he swiftly moves into my space and cups my jaw with his large hands as tenderly as possible. Then he kisses me. It's deep, it's hard, and it's full of meaning. Unfortunately, the meaning is goodbye. He separates from me and backs away.

"I think you're wrong, Jill, but if you don't want me, I won't beg. Just know that what we have between us doesn't come along very often, and you're throwing away something special. Goodbye, Jill."

"Johnny?"

He stops and waits, but never turns around. His hands are fisted in irritation, and his shoulders are tense. I don't know what to say so I stand there, freezing my butt off in the parking lot, wishing I were someone different, someone who deserves Johnny Browning and would be free to love him without issue. He tires of waiting for me to speak, so he gets in his truck and drives away, taking my heart with him.

PRAISE FOR AUTHOR

Tiffani Lynn

STRANGERS AT SUNSET

"Tiffani Lynn writes sexy, compelling stories with multi-dimensional characters, interesting plots, and hotter-than-hot sex! *Strangers at Sunset* immerses you in an emotional roller coaster of betrayal, discovery and acceptance—with a traditional happily-ever-after that melts the hearts of romance lovers everywhere. Five stars for a short but engaging read that introduces a new series from a new author who hit it out of the park."

~*Kat Mizera, author of The Sidewinder's series*

Dedication

To April, Lisa, Judy S., and Terri who have gone above and beyond to help make this dream come true for me. Without you, I'd be sitting in front of the first draft of the first story wondering which way is up. Saying thank you a million times is still not enough.

Author Acknowledgments

First and foremost, I need to acknowledge the sacrifice and support of my husband and daughters. Thank you for encouraging me to live my dream and for continuing to tell the world about my work.

Appreciation goes to my TLC crew, both husbands and wives. If it weren't for you guys helping with my kids in a multitude of ways, supporting my work, and making me laugh, there would be no books. I love you guys and treasure your special friendship. Don't forget, what you find is what you find!

Special thanks to my friends and family who help with my kids, entertain me, share my work, and hold my hand when things get rough. I'm incredibly blessed to have y'all in my life, and not a day goes by that I don't remember how lucky I am.

Donna Fiorentino, thank you for answering questions about your experience with breast cancer. Dawn Rogers, Connie King, Debra King, Leigh Anne Dearing, and Nina Smith, your strength is inspiring. Because of you, I will never miss a mammogram. To those near and dear to me who fought or continue to fight this horrible disease, it's an honor and a privilege to be part of your life.

Extra thanks go to fellow authors Lexi Post and Kat Mizera. Your advice, assistance, and support are priceless.

Judy Swinson, as always my gratitude goes to you for providing the tissues during the struggles and Snoopy-dancing alongside me for the accomplishments.

Last, but never least, my Beta Babes, Alison Dye, April Klusman, Barb Teeter, Barbie Stokes Timpson, Gemma Blomquist, Judy Swinson, Kat Mizera, Lisa Qualls, Maria Robinette, Rachel Garcia, and Terri Kuebbeler. I appreciate you taking time out of your busy lives to read my stories and share your thoughts. You ladies are amazing!

Prologue

I'm on the couch in the fetal position vacantly staring at Wheel of Fortune when Matt strolls through the door. It's been four days since I saw him last, and I've missed him. Any other day I'd be off the couch and in his arms, but after that pregnancy test popped up positive an hour ago, I haven't been able to do anything except feel sick to my stomach.

"Hey, Baby. You okay? You're a little pale." He places his palm against my forehead and then down over my cheek. He's attentive no matter what the situation is, so I don't know why I'm scared to tell him about the test. He's the one that keeps talking about marriage and a family. I know I'm not ready for any of that, but at the same time, the thought of carrying Matt's baby makes me feel like it might actually be okay in the end. I love him, and I know he loves me. My life has just been so hard up to this point, and I don't want to have a family and end up turning it into the sequel of my childhood.

"I've just had a bad day. I don't feel great either; I'm sorry. I've missed you. I wanted to make tonight nice."

"Well, don't you think you could shake it off? I haven't seen you in four days." He sounds a little annoyed. My brow furrows. Did he really just ask me that? I don't want to deal with moody Matt tonight. He gets like this from time to time, usually when I don't react the way he wants me to, or I say something he thinks is stupid. It's been a while since I've gotten the attitude, and I'm just not in the mood to deal with it tonight. Sometimes faking it is easier. Putting on a happy face all the time for him is exhausting, but I love him, so I do it to keep the peace. I'm just not sure if I can put on a show for him tonight.

"Matt, not every day with me is going to be sunny. Today has not been good. I missed you. Don't think I didn't, just give me a little bit to get out of this funk, okay?" I can hear the pleading tone in my voice, and I hate to sound like that, but I don't want to fight with him. He gives me a long hard look, his expression revealing nothing and walks out of the room.

Sighing I follow him into the bedroom and paste on a half-smile. "Want me to fix you something to eat?"

His gaze meets mine, and I can tell the instant he softens. The fine lines around his beautiful eyes disappear, and a faint smile appears on his face. He strides over to me and kisses me hard on the mouth.

"I ate on the road, so why don't we head to bed, and I'll give you a massage. Maybe that will get you in the mood." His grin grows, like that's all he's been thinking about while he was away, and I cringe a little inside because I am *not* in the mood, but I want to avoid a fight.

"Yeah, that sounds great."

He grabs my hands and propels me to the side of the bed. He's rough as he strips the clothes off my body and pushes me onto the bed. I slide backward to the middle. "Flip over so I can start on your back. I'm going to grab the oil, give me a second."

When he returns, he's stripped off all of his clothes except his boxers and is rubbing the vanilla-scented massage oil between his hands. I comply with his request and lay flat on my stomach with my arms at my sides, legs slightly apart, and my head turned to be able to watch him as he works. The muscles in his thighs flex as he leans over me, and I notice, not for the first time, how light his skin is in contrast to the wiry dark leg hairs that dust the skin. If this were any other day, I'd be dying to touch him when we're this close, but I'm just not up for it tonight.

His hands feel good on my tired, achy muscles, and in the back of my head, I convince myself that I can tell him my news in the morning, and it will all be okay.

After about twenty minutes, his fingers wander to the crack of my ass and down through the lips of my sex. As nice as that massage is, it doesn't do the trick. I roll half to my side so I can dislodge his hand and tell him, "I'm just not up for that tonight. The massage was great. I'm sorry; I know you're disappointed."

He gives me another long hard look and disappears into the bathroom. I hear the shower running for a while, and when he reemerges, he's wearing clean boxers. He doesn't say a word. He just lies on his side facing away from me. Damn, I'm really not in the mood for his sour attitude, but I don't want him mad either. I lay there debating about what to do for several long minutes until I finally give in and roll over to spoon against him and say, "I'm sorry, Matt. Please don't be mad. Tomorrow will be better."

He stays silent.

A few more minutes pass and the tears slip down my face as I whisper loud enough for him to hear, "I

3

love you, Matt."

I sniffle but stay silent where I am, waiting to see if he'll soften. When I'm certain we're at a stalemate for the night, I roll back to my side of the bed. The tears are rolling so fast down my face they're soaking my pillow. A few long minutes later, he pulls me into his arms and whispers, "I love you, too, Jill."

Not long after that, I fall asleep.

****

It's around six in the morning when I hear Matt in the bathroom slamming things around. That's not normal for him. Every other morning when he's here, he's quiet as he gets ready, very considerate.

About the time I'm realizing that his behavior in there doesn't sound normal, the door flies open and slams against the wall. The crunching sound upon impact signals a hole in the wall; I cringe.

His face is fierce. He's got an expression I've never seen on him. As I sit up to ask what's going on, he holds up the bag with the discarded box and pregnancy test and shakes it.

"I dumped a bunch of stuff in your trash, so I was going to change it for you instead of leaving it full and when I picked up the bag it had a hole in it. Guess what came tumbling out the bottom, Jill?"

My eyes widen, my mouth flaps open, and terror sharp and strong races through me from head to toe. He doesn't give me a chance to say anything else.

"When were you going to tell me, Jillian?" Angry isn't a good enough word for how he sounds. The tone of his voice is reminiscent of one my father uses often with me, and he's never been anything but cruel to me. My body begins to tremble in fear.

"Today," I answer quietly.

"Why didn't you tell me last night, Jill? This is pretty important news. Is this why you weren't feeling good? You lied to me." His voice is cold, distant, and so unlike anything I've heard from him before.

"I was scared. I just wanted you to hold me. I wanted to build up the courage. I'm still scared." I probably sound like a little girl—quiet, hesitant, terrified.

"You should be. This is fucked up. Are you trying to trap me? You think you can force me to marry you because you got knocked up? This isn't 1955, Jillian. Just because you get knocked up doesn't mean I have to marry you."

He paces the small bedroom. His hands clench and the lines in his forehead deepen as his irritation seems to grow. "Why? Why would you do this to me?"

"Do this to you? I don't understand what you mean?" I scoot to the edge of the bed and pull the sheet up as high as I can get it.

"Of course you know what I mean. You're trying to trap me."

My fear is morphing into anger, and it's burning low in my belly. I slide off the bed and tug a T-shirt over my head to hide the nakedness that has me feeling more vulnerable than I'd like.

"I didn't *do* this to you. It was a mistake. I'm not even sure how it happened. I never missed a pill. I wasn't even certain that I wanted kids at all, much less right now. Why do you think I planned this? Have I ever made you think I was rushing things with us? No. I'm usually the one putting on the brakes. You've been the one to talk about marriage. Not me. Why would you

5

think I did this on purpose?"

I tug a pair of panties on while he levels me with a cold gaze, meant to intimidate.

"I know all about chicks like you." He spits the words, hate rolling off his tongue while his finger jabs the air in front of him.

"Dating a guy with a college degree and a good job hoping to make him marry you. So you can have him take care of you and pay your fucking bills. No. Way. You need to call the abortion clinic. You're *not* keeping this baby. No. Fucking. Way!" Loud and angry, his voice echoes off the walls of my tiny apartment.

"You don't get to decide that alone, Matt." I stride over, plant my feet right in front of him, and glare. His beautiful face is contorted like an angry troll, so I muster up my best look of defiance before I say, "I don't think I could kill our baby. I may not have planned this, but it's happening, and if you don't want to be a part of this, then walk out that door. I've been surviving on my own for the last six years. I'm sure I can make this work, too."

I'm trying to be bold and stand up for our unborn child and myself. That's what mothers are supposed to do, right? The problem is that I'm a little afraid he might really do that as I finish this sentence. On the other hand, I'm fired up that he accused me of doing this on purpose.

He tilts his head to the side as his gaze narrows on me. "Are you telling me that you refuse to get rid of it?"

"Yes. I am. If you'd have discussed this with me rationally, then I might be able to see your point of view, but you've just accused me of trying to trap you and then told me to kill *our* baby. Don't you get that this is *our* baby? Part of you and part of me?" I gesture between the two of us.

We've had a few fights over the last year when he starts acting selfish, but most of the time I back down and either apologize or just try to smooth things over. I hate fighting with him, but he's never been quite this horrible before, and I'm reeling in shock.

I grip his shirt in my fists as I plead with him. "What the hell, Matt? Why would you say those things? You know I do whatever you want me to do, whenever you want me to do it. How can you be so cruel? Were you saving all of your venom for this one special day?"

"Fuck you, Jill!" he screams as he wrenches my hands from his shirt and backs away. "You have no idea what you've done by forcing a kid on me. I wanted to take it slow with you, because I *never* intended on getting married or having kids. I like you, Jillian, but I don't see a future for us. I've only ever seen a right now, and I think even that is over."

He should have just punched me in the throat. It would have shocked and hurt me less. I knew he'd be angry, but breaking up with me? I didn't see that coming.

The anger I've been trying to keep at a low level boils over the top. "You *like* me? *Like* me? You love me was the last thing you said to me last night!" I shriek at him.

My body is past shaking from fear and is now vibrating with anger and hurt. I can't believe what I'm hearing come out of his mouth. "For the last six months, you've told me every day how much you love me, and that you want to marry me. But now you *like* me? I didn't expect you to be doing cartwheels about having a baby, but I had no idea you'd do a complete one-eighty on me."

"If I *really* loved you, I'd be here with you every night. Not a couple of days every week. If I *really* loved you, I'd have asked you to marry me already, not just mentioned it in passing. How damn stupid can you be, Jill? You've just been a placeholder for the last year. It was never going to be anything else. Trying to force it by getting knocked up only ended things quicker than I planned."

I feel like he's delivering physical blows with each word. One after the other. The bile is climbing up my throat as rivers of tears run down my face. Who is this man? It's not the same man that pursued me with unrelenting tenacity, or the same man that made love to me a thousand times.

"You know what Matt? *Fuck! You!*" I screech at the top of my lungs.

Self-control? Gone.

Fear? Gone.

Replacement? Blinding rage.

"Fuck you for lying to me, for using me, and for thinking I'd even want a future with you. I'm glad you don't want our baby. I'd never want it to grow up knowing what kind of fucked up father it had! I loved every ounce of you, every part you've ever shown me, even your little mood swings when you don't get your way. But now I know you're a hateful, heartless asshole. I've given you everything I am, everything I've got and you just shit on me. Leave. If it's over… Get. The fuck. Out of my house. Now!"

He stands still for a whole minute watching me

shake and cry. He shutters his expression, and I'm no longer able to see anger or hate. I can see nothing. I'm not sure what he's thinking. The blank expression makes my blood run cold. He's dead serious about everything he's said. This isn't some lover's spat, that much is clear. How did I miss that about him for a whole year? Was he that good an actor, or was I just being naïve?

I was afraid he'd be upset when he found out because this wasn't planned. Hell, I was upset about it, but I didn't realize he would morph into a complete stranger. This was a man I've only had glimpses of before, and he beat the emotional crap out of me. He just tore up anything beautiful I've ever had in my life with his words. I'm not sure I'm going to survive it.

He turns around without uttering another word and strides out of my apartment. Instead of chasing him, I rush to the bathroom and throw up the contents of my stomach in the toilet. When I'm done, I just lie on the floor right where I'm at and cry for hours. The anger fades and is once again replaced by hurt. He's left an ache so deep you could dig for a week and never get to the heart of it.

He never comes back. The last vision I have of Matt is his back as he strides out the door.

Chapter One

Jill

It's been six months since I found out I was pregnant, and a lot has changed. After a few months of waitressing, I wasn't able to fit into the uniform so I quit and got a job as a janitor at a nursing home. It's hard work and long hours, but they give me overtime often, and I've been able to stash some cash into savings.

Florida is calling my name. Living near the ocean has always been a dream of mine, and now with nothing holding me here, I plan to use the extra cash to move once the baby is born. Everything I've read says that the cost of living is cheaper, there is no state tax on wages, and the tourist-heavy cities have better employment rates for blue-collar workers. I also won't have to worry about scraping snow and ice off my car or buying snow tires.

I've decided to notify Matt of my change of location and let him know how sorry I am about how everything went down. I hate him for using me all that time and treating me like crap that last day, but he *is* her father. He may not want to know his daughter now, but someday he may change his mind, and I want him to be able to find her if that happens. I'd given up on the idea of a life with him after he walked out the door on me that last morning and never returned, but not the hope that he'd want to know our daughter. He must have meant the things he said though, because he never attempted to contact me after that. He even left all of his stuff behind. I think that surprised me the most.

In my heart, I want to see him one more time. I need to convince myself that our time together was real because right now I'm so alone that this feels like an immaculate conception. As much as I still love him, I couldn't be with a person like that after growing up in the house I did, but it doesn't stop my heart from hurting.

I've waited until now to approach him because I wanted to be strong when I did. The first several months after he left, I was an absolute mess. I'm stronger now and feel like I can handle this. I don't want to wait until after she's born, because I don't want to subject her to his words or actions if they're nasty. To be quite honest, I'm still expecting them to be unpleasant, but I feel like he needs to know how to find her.

I've already loaded the box of all the stuff he left here, so I grab the address from beside the computer and the directions I printed off the Internet and head out the door. I gave up my smart phone and got an old flip phone that I only plan to use in case of emergency, because it saves me over a hundred dollars a month. That extra money has gone into the savings account for our move, but giving up that technology has me doing a lot of things the old fashioned way.

After two hours on the road, I arrive at the address that the Internet lists as Matt's house. It's Friday, and I plan to check in to an old motel up the street from his house for a few days if he's not home yet. I know he

used to come back here at least once a week, and I'm
pretty sure it was on the weekend. If I have to, I'll wait.
I will talk to him one way or the other.

It's six-thirty in the evening when I turn in to the
driveway. There is a streetlight standing next to his
mailbox. It lights up the front of the house making the
house number next to the garage more visible.

When the sun sets, the March wind seems so much
colder, and I tug my sweater tighter across my swollen
belly and stare at the cute gray two-story house with
black shutters and a classic front porch with a swing.
It's not at all what I expected for the eternal bachelor.
There's a black Honda Accord in the driveway and a
light on in the front window. It appears that he's home.
He must have gotten a new car, a new girlfriend, or
maybe both.

I wobble up to the front door in all my pregnant
roundness and ring the bell. My hands are shaking a
little. I'm wishing he wouldn't have shut his phone off.
This would have been easier for me to do over the
phone. I say a little prayer in my head that things don't
get as nasty as the day he found out. I'm rubbing my
hands together nervously in front of me when the door
opens. A gorgeous woman stands in the doorway
wiping her hands off on a dishtowel. She has a mass of
beautiful, curly blonde hair that hangs several inches
past her shoulders. I think her eyes are blue, but it's
hard to tell in the limited amount of light. She's a
couple of inches taller than I am, and I know right away
this is Matt's new woman. Jealousy zips through me,
and I take a deep breath at the unexpected pain of the
idea. No wonder he never came back for me. He moved
on, and she is stunning.

I remind myself that he's a bastard, and I shouldn't care. Maybe I shouldn't have come. Why did I think this was a good idea? Oh lord, I think I'm going to be sick.

The woman gives me a tentative smile. "Can I help you?"

My voice is shaky when I ask, "Hi, is Matt here?" I'm wishing I'd never have come here, but I can't chicken out now. I need to try to at least talk to him. The expression on her face changes in an instant and tears well up in her eyes.

"I'm sorry, but Matt died back in September."

I swear to all that is holy, the bottom drops out from underneath me. My head spins a little and my legs turn to jelly.

I must have passed out because my eyes open to see an unfamiliar ceiling. I peek around at the foreign but comfortable surroundings in an attempt to figure out where I am. It's then that I come face to face with the lips of a fawn-colored Boxer dog. He's resting his head on the cushion my head is laid out on, and his warm doggie breath is snuffling across my face. Over the dog's head, I see the blonde lady again, and everything comes rushing back. I sit up straight, causing my head to spin again. My heart starts pounding, and my breathing becomes fast and shallow. Sensing I'm going to pass out again, the lady approaches me and urges me to lie back down. This is awkward.

"Matt's dead? Really dead? You're not telling me this so I'll go away?" I question in a high, nervous voice.

Her forehead wrinkles as her eyebrows lift up to her hairline. She shakes her head. "Why would I do that?" Her head jerks back a little, and her eyes narrow on me.

"Because I'm having his baby. He didn't want it. I thought he'd abandoned us." I rush the words out in a breathy panic.

The lady falls back on her ass and scurries away like a crab. Now she's the one hyperventilating. Her dog who was sitting near me on the floor is now at her side, nudging her with his face.

"Wh-Wh-What are y-y-you t-talking about?" she stutters out, shocked.

"I was Matt's girlfriend. He dumped me and flipped out when he found out that I'm having his baby. He found out back in September, but I'm due in about a month. I just wanted to let him know that we are moving. If he decided he wanted to see her, our daughter, he'd need to know where we moved to."

My insides are cramping up. I'm tense. I know something isn't right with this situation, but my brain is not working out whatever it is.

"Matt can't be the father of your baby. He's been my husband for over ten years. We've been together for over fifteen years. Never broken up. Not once. Only been with each other. You must be mistaken. You must have the wrong Matt. Here let me show you my Matt. It's not the same Matt."

She jumps up, rushing now, panic-stricken. I'm praying she can prove me wrong, but if it's the same guy, everything makes sense now. All the nights he spent away from me, never bringing me to his home and never introducing me to his family. It's why he was so mad and why he said he never wanted anything more than what we had.

She passes me a picture of him that she says was taken just over a year ago at one of his work functions, and one of them on their wedding day to show me. He's much younger and his hair is longer in the wedding picture, but it is the same Matt. The work function picture looks just like Matt the first night I saw him. His beautiful, charismatic smile spread across his handsome face caught on film and staring right back at me with his arm around the blonde woman whose house I'm in. This is the same Matt who told me he loved me. The one who helped create the baby I carry in my womb. Also the same Matt who said he only liked me and never planned to marry me. It all hits me like a freight train. A roaring starts in my ears, and the room feels stuffy. I clutch at my throat as I gasp for air and black out again.

This time when I wake up, I find the woman, Matt's wife, sitting on the floor beside me. She's crying hard, her body shaking with sobs, and I just want to die with the realization of it all. This is the worst day of my life. Worse than when my parents beat me to a bloody pulp with a switch. Worse than when I found my brother dead by his own hand. Worse than the day Matt left me. I've just ruined this woman's life and in turn ruined my own.

Not only is Matt a user and a liar, but also a cheater. He's dead. He died about the same time I told him about the baby. I'd like to know when exactly, but I know this is not the person to ask or the right time.

I stand up knowing that I need to get out of here, but I'm so big and uncomfortable that I look awkward and ridiculous.

"I'm so sorry. I'm so sorry. I didn't know he was

married. I didn't know he was dead. I swear I didn't know."

I'm hysterical now, darting around the room searching for my purse and my keys. I have to leave. I have to get the hell out of here. I'm going to be sick or I'm going to pass out again. I can't do this. I can't believe I showed up here and hurt this poor woman. What the hell was I thinking? Her dog is watching me with cautious eyes. It's almost as if he knows I've come unhinged in his house, and he has no idea how to handle that.

She stands up, wipes her eyes, and in an eerily calm voice says, "I get that you're pregnant, and you've just found out that Matt is dead. I don't know what to do with any of this information, and to be frank, I don't know what to do about you. I can't believe you're pregnant and saying it's Matt's. I can't believe you're in my living room. I can't think about it right now. Please write your number down, and I'll call you in a few days. If this is true, we have a lot to talk about. I just, I just…can't do it now. My name is Lisa. I'll call you when I can."

She leaves a pen and paper on the coffee table and strides up the stairs with her dog at her heels. Then I hear the bang of a door when she gets upstairs followed by a blood-curdling scream, and the sound of glass and metal smashing. I write down my name and number and leave her home.

I shouldn't be driving. I have to stop three times to throw up before I get on the interstate, but I want to go home. I need to crawl into my bed and stay there. I might be in shock; I'm not sure how I made it this far. A glance at the clock tells me I've been driving for close to two hours. I realize I'm somewhere outside of Indianapolis when a car changes lanes without checking his blind spot, and I'm too spaced out to notice until it's too late. He smashes into me, jarring my whole body, running me off the road. I lose control of the car and black out as it flips over.

****

Blinking rapidly a few times, I try to focus on the bright fluorescent lights coming into view. I squint and try to acclimate my eyes. Turning my head to the left, I see medical equipment. A bunch of it. I can hear a whooshing sound and something that sounds like blips. I turn my head to the right and see an empty hospital bed. My leg muscles ache, kind of like they do when I've stayed in one position too long. I try to move them, but that just hurts worse. I wince and attempt to bend my arms, which I can't see because the blanket is pulled almost all the way up to my chin. My right arm feels heavy, like cement blocks are attached. I try the other arm and it moves, but it aches so badly I cringe. I slide it out from under the blankets and realize it's covered in purple bruises and several angry scrapes. That explains the aches. I use it to lift the blanket on the other side and find that I have a cast on the lower part of my arm. That explains the cement feeling, but how did I get like this? I have no idea and the lack of knowledge incites panic.

I freak out. My heart rate increases to the point that it feels like it's going to jump out of my chest. Breathing is difficult all of a sudden. The beeping in the background seems to get louder. I have no idea how I got here. I'm pregnant, and it's obvious something happened to me.

Is my baby okay? I move my hands to my stomach hoping to find the round, taut skin I've been rubbing for months. It's there but covered by something. I can't get the hospital gown up to see what it is. What the hell is going on? I start pressing any button I can touch on the box that's clipped to my blanket. The television pops on, the volume goes up, and back down. Then a voice says to me, "This is the nurse. How can I help you?"

I drop the little box and peer around to see where the sound is coming from, but I can't find it. Maybe I'm going crazy.

"How can I help you?" The voice repeats.

Where is it coming from?

"Where am I? Is my baby okay?"

Panic floods my system. My brain is whirling both with a dizzy sensation and questions, too many questions.

"Help. Help! What's going on?"

I'm thrashing now, and with every movement, it feels like needles in my ribs. The IV in my arm pinches, but that is nothing compared to how bad I hurt all over.

A short, stout, African American woman rushes into the room.

"It's okay, Jillian. You're okay. Your baby is okay. You've got to calm down though. She's not going to stay in there and finish growing if you get upset, all right? Settle down and I'll explain. Do you need some water?" Her voice is soothing, sweet and has the desired effect of calming me with every word.

As a matter of fact, I do. It feels like cotton has been stuffed into my cheeks. My throat is like sandpaper. I nod a yes. She pours a little water in a cup, puts the straw in, and holds it up for me. Realizing that this won't work, she presses a button to raise the head of the bed and then gives me my sip.

After a few of those, when she's certain I've calmed down, she tells me everything.

"I'm Veronica, your daytime nurse. You were in an accident on the interstate two nights ago. It was bad. You're lucky to be alive and only have minimal injuries. Your car flipped four times the witnesses said. You're a living miracle, young lady. It's also amazing that your baby is okay. The only problem for you is that you'll be on bed rest for a couple of weeks, maybe longer. We're going to keep you here and monitor you until you can be induced. Your labor started in the life flight helicopter on the way here, which is too early for her. So we're going to keep things low key for you."

****

Two days later my cell phone rings from the bedside table where the police left it for me.

"Hello?"

"Jill, this is Lisa Browning, Matt's wife." She sounds cordial but curt.

I feel a little stab in my heart at the word wife.

"Hi."

"I don't want to be rude, but I don't see another way than to just ask you straight out. Once the baby is born, are you willing to submit to a DNA test?"

"I'm confused. Why would I want to do that? I know who this baby's parents are."

I can hear her exhale on the other end.

"If you're planning on getting a piece of his estate then I'll require a DNA test. I have a hairbrush of his I haven't touched, so I can use that for his sample."

"I didn't come to find him that day for money. I

came to find him to tell him I was moving. I was hoping he'd eventually want to be a part of her life and come to find her. Now that I know that isn't a possibility, I'm not asking for anything. I'll raise this baby on my own."

"What about Matt's family? They're going to want to know they have a granddaughter."

"I don't know them, and I don't care to if they're anything like Matt. He was cruel, and he used me up and spit me out. He lied to me and promised things he never planned on following through with. He had to have learned it from somewhere."

"Matt's family is some of the nicest, most loving people I've ever met, and the man you're describing is not my Matt." Sounds like I've hit a sensitive spot for her.

"Well, since we both know I am talking about the same Matt, I think it's clear you didn't know him like you thought you did. Just like I didn't know him. I'm sorry I ever showed up on your doorstep. I honestly didn't know he was married. I didn't mean to hurt you. I won't bother you again." My words are rushed. I'm trying to avoid breaking down on the phone with her, but my gut is churning and my eyes are filling up.

"If you decide to submit to a DNA test I'll be glad to talk to you again. Until then, I guess this is goodbye." Her voice ends quieter than it did a minute ago, and I'm hit once again with a wave of regret for all of this.

"I guess so."

We both hang on the line, neither of us pressing 'end'. It's awkward, but I can tell she has more to say.

"Can I ask you a couple of questions?"

I exhale a little louder than is normal. "Yes, it depends on what they are if I'll answer them."

"How did you meet him? How long were you together?"

"He came into the bar I worked at and asked me out every night for a week straight. I finally said yes on night eight, and we were together for about a year when he left. He ended things when he found out about the baby. He said I was trying to trap him. He asked me to abort her. I refused. He never once said he was married. He traveled for work, and then he'd come back to me on his off nights. I've never gotten much out of relationships, so I didn't think to question his frequent absences or him never taking me to Cincinnati to meet his family. I should've known. When and how did he die? I never got to ask."

"Massive heart attack. In our living room. September 5th."

"That was just three days after I told him about the baby. I'm really sorry, Lisa."

It's silent for several seconds and then her throat clears. "Okay, I'll let you go. If you decide to take the test just call me on this number and we'll work out the details.

"Thank you, but don't count on it. I never wanted anything from him except for him to love his daughter, and that's the truth. I'm sorry for your loss."

"Goodbye, Jill."

"Goodbye, Lisa."

I hang up the phone and cry until I fall asleep.

My parents also come to visit and after giving me a nasty tongue-lashing, disown me for spawning Satan's child. Their words, not mine. The rest of my time in the hospital is boring and after a month, I deliver my beautiful baby girl, Mariah. During the delivery, I have complications, which of course prolong my hospital stay. After six weeks, I'm able to return home and after another six weeks, I'm able to go back to work.

Catching up on all the bills that piled up in my absence is hell. Because I didn't work for three months, I have to clear my savings account out to cover the bills. I'd let my car insurance lapse a day before the accident without realizing it, and the guy who hit me ran, so I had no one to cover the damage to my car. I have to use the last fifteen hundred dollars in my account to get an old piece of junk to get me to work and Mariah to daycare. My hope of moving to Florida is now a distant memory.

As I reach the top step, hands full of car seat and baby paraphernalia, I see the rent due notice on my door. I'm more than just one month late and have no way to cover it. After reading the notice, I do what I never wanted to do and call Lisa Browning, Matt's wife, to let her know that I will consent to the paternity test. If I don't get help from Matt's estate, Mariah and I will be on the streets within the month.

****

Johnny

Lisa just left Mom and Dad's house. She dropped a bomb on our family tonight with news about my brother having a daughter. Let me clarify: my brother the asshole, Matt, not Steve. It shouldn't shock me. He always was the most selfish of the three of us boys, but this is taking it to a new level. Steve was so pissed he stormed out. My parents and sister never seemed to notice Matt's narcissistic ways, but Steve and I saw it plenty. He could be a real dickhead when he felt like it. Of course, my parents might as well have put a crown on him and called him sire with the big deal they made about every single thing he did. I'm sure their shock is greater than mine. I feel bad for Lisa more than anything. She's a wonderful woman and had always been one hundred percent devoted to Matt. She didn't deserve any of this shit.

A girlfriend and a four-month-old baby is what Lisa said. You could've knocked me over with a feather after she told us. I know my mom will call Jill. If she doesn't, my dad will. They've both been ready for grandkids for a couple of years now, but none of us has any kids yet. I'm sure they will also see this as a way to hold onto their *Golden Child.*

Lisa mentioned that Matt cheated with more than one woman. I wonder how many she meant, and if she knows about all of them. My brother has a kid. Wow. Just thinking that is messing with my head. As pissed as I am at Matt, I'd still like a chance to get to know this newly-found niece. One thing that has always been important to all of us Brownings is family, and this little girl is one of us, so I'm hoping to have some kind of relationship with her. I'm hoping her mother is the kind of person to allow that. I can't imagine what she thinks of all of us knowing what kind of man Matt was. Something tells me that life around here is about to get really interesting.

****

A few days later, while at work, my phone rings, and the caller I.D. shows that it's my brother.

"Hey, Steve. What's up?"

He sounds a little irritated when he answers, "Dad

just called. He needs us to take off of work to bring Jill and the baby back to Cincinnati."

"What are you talking about?" I'm confused. I knew they were going to meet the girl and their granddaughter, but I never heard anything about her coming home with them.

"Things are bad for Jill in Indy, and Dad is insisting she move in with them. You know Dad, if it doesn't seem right he'll take over. Especially now that his grandbaby is involved."

"So why do we need to take off?" I can't figure out why I need to take off of work, too, for this.

He's exasperated that I'm not getting it. "To help move her stuff here. You know Dad can't do that by himself. I don't want to use vacation days to help a home wrecker, but Dad gave me hell about it, so we need to go."

"It must be bad for Dad to call you. I don't mind going. I'm curious about what we're walking into, but if that's what Dad wants I'll be there. I can pick you up about six in the morning, if you want me to drive my truck. We may need it."

"Okay, that sounds good. I'll be ready." I hear him let out a puff of air.

"Try to calm down. We don't know anything about this girl. We have no idea if she knew he was married or not. Try to keep an open mind until we know more. It'll be important to Mom and Dad. If it helps Mom deal with everything better, then I'm all for it."

"I can't promise you anything, but I'll try. I don't want to upset Mom and Dad."

"Lisa wanted us to have a relationship with the baby, too; it's the whole reason she told us about Jill, so keep that in mind. Let's just do what Dad wants and get her moved here. We can deal with anything else later. I'll see you bright and early."

"All right, see you tomorrow."

We hang up and I notify the manager that he's in charge of the automotive shop that I own while I'm gone tomorrow.

Chapter Two

Jill

A week and a half later, I get a call from my lawyer, Frank Bennett. He's the cheapest one I could find. I'm not fond of the guy, but I had no choice in the matter.

"Hello?"

"Hello, Jill? It's Frank Bennett. Can you talk?" He sounds excited.

"Yes, go ahead."

"The results came back positive, and they have made an offer."

"Already? I figured it would take time for all of that." I know I sound skeptical, but it's been my experience that if something seems too good to be true it probably is.

"Yes, it's a pretty good one, too. If it were me, I'd take it, but it's up to you. First, they plan to pay off your medical bills from the birth. We figured those to be about a hundred and fifty thousand dollars. Then the offer is six hundred a month every month until the baby's eighteen, retroactive to the date of her birth. She'll get fifty thousand dollars for college or trade school. Then receive half of the remainder of the trust at age twenty-five and the other half at age thirty, unless that money has to be tapped into for other things. There are also provisions for serious illness and major accidents. In a case like that, we'll be able to petition the executor of the trust for funds to pay her medical bills. The executor is Mark Willis, Mrs. Browning's attorney. We can fight it and ask for more, or we can take it and be thankful. The lump sum of the whole package is exactly half of Matthew Browning's estate. I can ask for more a month, which would drop the payouts at twenty-five and thirty years old to less, but would help more now. What do you want me to do?"

I'm speechless. I can't believe she's being so generous especially considering the situation. I'm not stupid or greedy and the old saying about looking a gift horse in the mouth comes to mind.

"Yes, I accept it. It's very generous. I don't want to be greedy and ask for more a month. I should be able to make that work. What do you need from me?"

"Just come by my office today if possible. I need you to sign some paperwork. It should all be taken care of so you can get your first check in the next couple of weeks."

"Thank you, Mr. Bennett." Tears fill my eyes that I'm thankful no one can see.

"You're welcome, Jill. I'm glad this process has been relatively easy for you. It's not always this easy."

"Thank you again for everything, I'll see you later today."

I hang up the phone, flabbergasted that Lisa has been so generous. I may be able to make things work this way. I hope that the first check shows up before I get evicted. I wish there were some way to properly thank her for doing this. I'm sure she could have fought me and won, never having to give anything up, but she didn't.

****

Two weeks later, I am sitting on the couch holding Mariah. It's quiet in our little apartment. The hum of the refrigerator and soft baby snores are all I can hear. She's all cuddled up in my arms asleep. The scent of her sweet baby lotion-covered skin floats up to my nose as I stroke the dark curly hair coming in all over her pretty little round head. Her small chubby fist is wrapped around the collar of my shirt. I'm relishing this moment. I don't usually have time to just sit and enjoy motherhood, but I made some time today. I felt like we needed it. I could watch her for hours as she sleeps. Her little lips are pulling and working her pacifier like she's eating. It's the cutest thing ever. Then the shrill ring of my cell phone interrupts the sweet moment.

Only a handful of people have this number, and I can't figure out why any of them would be calling. Curious, I pick it up, answering quietly so I don't scare my girl.

"Hello?"

"Is this Jillian Pierce?" It's a woman's voice.

"Yes, this is Jill. Who am I speaking with?"

"This is Matthew Browning's mom, Judy. Please don't hang up." She sounds nervous.

"I won't. How did you get my number?"

"Lisa. Lisa told us about the baby and said we should call." Her words are rushed like she's scared.

"Really? Is this a joke?" My voice is heavy with the cynicism I'm feeling.

"Oh, no, honey! Not at all. I know this is strange under the circumstances, but if the information is true, I'd like to meet you and my granddaughter. I can't imagine Lisa would lie about something like this."

"I'm not sure it's a good idea. I can't imagine what you must think of me, but I didn't know he was married. He never told me—" She cuts me off.

"No, no. I'm not calling to judge or ask questions. I'd honestly like to meet you both. My whole family would: my husband, my two sons, my daughter, and their spouses. I promise not to cause trouble for you. Please think about it. We can come to you, or I can fly you here. Lisa said you live in Indianapolis. Is that right?"

"Yes, ma'am, I do. I work a lot and only have one day off at a time, never two in a row. Do you think you could come here? Maybe just you and your husband to start, and we could go from there. To be honest, I'm a little freaked out. Life and people haven't been very kind to me, and I'm having a hard time understanding why you'd want us in your life."

"I can understand that. I don't know the details, but I do know there is a part of my son still left in this world, and I'd like to be part of her life, however you'll allow it to happen. I also know you were with him for a year; it wasn't a one-night-stand, so I'm certain my son saw something in you worth knowing. I'd like the opportunity to find out what that is. When is it best for us to visit? You tell me the day and time, and my husband and I will be there. We'd actually like to stay in a hotel nearby for a couple of days. We won't interfere with your schedule; we'd just like to spend a little time getting to know you both."

I hesitate, not sure what to say at first, then I blurt out, "I'm off of work the day after tomorrow. Mariah is usually up by seven o'clock, so you can come any time after eight. Is that too soon?"

"No, that would be great. Can we take you to breakfast?"

"That would be lovely. We'll go when you get here. Mariah has her morning nap about ten o'clock, so if we can work around that it would be great."

"We'll be there at eight." She sounds happy.

I give her my address before we disconnect and wonder what in the world this is all about. Why would Lisa Browning give my number to Matt's parents? I figured she'd have a voodoo doll with my name on it and pins sticking out of it instead of sending grandparents my way.

I'm nervous to meet these people. Judy seemed nice, but I thought Matt was, too, and he ended up being cruel and heartless. What if they treat me like my own parents? I don't think I can take any more beat downs.

****

Two days later, a short, roundish woman with brown hair, brilliant green eyes, and a kind smile stands at my front door along with a tall man who is an aged replica of Matt. His eyes match Matt's and Mariah's. Seeing his dad almost does me in. In an instant, my knees get weak, my eyes tear up, and my breath leaves me for places unknown.

"Oh my God. You look just like him," I whisper, fingers over my mouth. Mariah is in my arms chewing on her fist, making gurgling noises, unaware of the drama unfolding.

Judy gives me a warm smile. "One of Matt's brothers does, too, more so actually. Hi, I'm Judy." She puts her hand out in front of her to shake mine, and I take it. Her hand is soft and warm, and her smile is timid but genuine.

She glances down at Mariah and tears up. I smile back. I'm nervous, but I try not to let it show as I usher them inside and wave them toward the couch. I offer them a drink, and they decline.

Finally, I sit down in a small chair across from them and perch Mariah on my lap. She's going to town on her fist, and drool is running down the front of her. Their eyes are intent as they watch us, and I can tell by the expressions on Judy and John's faces that they now realize she has Matt's eyes, those beautiful whiskey-colored eyes. Judy lets out a sob, and John puts his arm around her, pulling her in close. I can hear him telling her with a tenderness I've never experienced, "It's okay, baby. We knew this was going to be hard, but it's going to be okay. I love you, and we can do this together."

She sniffles, wipes her eyes, and pastes a smile back on her face.

Tentatively, she asks, "Can I…maybe…hold her?"

I respond with more enthusiasm than I feel. It seems strange handing my baby over to another woman. I do it every day at daycare, but this feels different. I force myself to relax and say, "Of course you can. Let me wipe her face, and I'll hand her over."

They wait while I clean her up. My hands shake the entire time, even when I lift her into Judy's arms. Mariah studies both of them with a serious expression for a moment and then gives the biggest gummy smile she has in her arsenal to them. Now I see John's eyes glisten with unshed tears as he squeezes Judy's shoulder.

Judy smiles back at her and says, "She's beautiful,

Jill, a wonderful mix of both of you. She's so chunky and healthy. I love babies with a little meat on their bones. All of my kids were that way. Is she a good baby?"

"The best. She doesn't fuss unless she's hungry. She sleeps through the night, or at least she has for the last two and a half months. She's meeting all of her baby milestones right on time. She's a blessing."

"She sure is. Thank you for letting us come here. I can't tell you how much it means to us."

"You're welcome."

****

John and Judy spend that whole day and the next evening with us after I get off work. I was really nervous at first but have slowly started to relax. Their intentions are clear. They just want to get to know Mariah and want to be a part of our lives. It's been kind of nice having someone around to help. After a long day at work, a second set of hands is a Godsend. Tomorrow is the last day they will be here, but they plan to come back next month and visit us again. They treated us to dinner at Bubba's BBQ and are now returning to my apartment to visit a little bit longer before they have to leave. As we are ascending the stairs, I catch sight of another pink sticker and the smile I've had on my face since yesterday fades from my lips. It's attached to an envelope with my name written on it, which is taped to the door. I know what that is. Mortification slides through me from top to toe like someone injected it into my veins. I'm so embarrassed that this had to show up when his parents are here. I could crawl under a rock and die. Seriously. Die.

I yank it off the door, and usher everyone inside. I

need to see what the exact dates are before the hysteria sets in. I'm pretty sure I know the answer already, but I'm praying for a miracle. I need time. I'm still a couple of weeks away from getting the check from Matt's estate. I hand the baby to Judy and grip the envelope in my hand.

John stays by my side and asks in his deep voice, "What is that? I can tell it's not good."

"Honestly? I haven't read it, but I'm certain it's an eviction notice. I fell behind when Mariah was born. It's a long story, but I was in the hospital for over a month, and then I couldn't go back to work for another six weeks so I got behind, and I just can't catch up. I depleted my savings buying a car and trying to keep up with the bills while not getting a pay check."

His eyebrows push low and he asks, "What happened to the money Lisa gave you?"

"I haven't received any of it yet. I'm a couple of weeks away from getting the first check. It will be okay. I just have to talk to the landlord."

I know it's not going to be okay, because the landlord said once the envelope shows up I have about seventy-two hours to vacate or they lock me out, without our stuff. I don't tell John that, though; I'm embarrassed by this whole situation.

Judy speaks up from the living room. "Are your parents around, honey?"

"No. My parents are religious zealots. They told me that Mariah was Satan's child and disowned me for being pregnant with her."

I swear I hear John growl and Judy gasp.

"Who's helping you with everything, Jill?" John asks rather gruffly.

"No one." I answer him quietly, wishing we could end this line of questioning. "I don't have anyone. No family. No friends. I'm getting some government assistance to help with Mariah's essentials and daycare costs. That will last until the checks start coming in from Matt's estate. At that point, I was told I'd be making too much money to keep getting help. We'll be okay though. I've made it this far."

John stands in front of me with hands on his hips. He bows his head and allows the silence to grow between us, just long enough to make me uncomfortable. "Jill, normally I wouldn't act like this around someone I just met, but I'm about to get a bit bossy, and I expect you to listen. I'm not doing it to be rude or take over your life, but whether you like it or not, you're a part of our family now, and we take care of our own. Now pass me the envelope. I'd like to see what it says for myself."

What he says shocks me. Shame continues to sit heavy in my gut, but I can't hide any of it, so I just pass the letter over to him.

He reads it, curses under his breath and inquires, "Are you determined to stay in this town?"

Shaking my head, I say, "No, I planned to move to Florida once she was born. I researched and found the cost of living is cheaper down there. I was going to use my savings to pay for the move. I thought it would be easier on me, but I haven't been able to get out from under the financial mess here yet."

"Jill, I'm not sure how, but we'll help you. Give me a little bit to think about it, okay?"

I open my mouth to protest and get the evil eye from him.

"Don't try to argue with me. Just give me some time to think about it."

Half an hour later, John and Judy leave for their hotel, and Mariah and I go to bed. That night sleep eludes me. I'm terrified we'll be homeless. Even if it's for a short while, I don't think I can deal with that.

After a long day at work, I pick up Mariah and meet the Brownings at my apartment. After we have the baby in her highchair and Judy has taken over feeding her dinner, John says, "I'm thinking you need to move to Cincinnati, at least for now. We'll be able to help you with Mariah and a place to live if you'll let us. You can either live with us until you're ready to be on your own again, or we can put you up in a hotel nearby while we look for a place of your own. Judy and I talked about it last night and want to help you. Either option is fine with us. Cincinnati's a nice town, a family town. Matt's two brothers and his sister could help, too. If I thought you had all of that here, I'd never say a word, but young lady, you need family around you, people who care about you, who are willing to help out."

Between the feelings of embarrassment, sadness, and appreciation, I turn into a blubbering basket case. I drop down hard in the chair at the kitchen table and sob. No one has ever said anything like that to me. Ever. No one has ever cared about helping me.

It seems too good to be true. Can I trust these people to help me? Or will it be another version of Matt? I don't think I'd survive that again. I just don't have any other options left. It's either get help from them or sleep on the streets with my baby.

I pick my head up, eyes seeking my daughter only to find her smiling like a lunatic as Judy feeds her, and I realize, like everything else lately, it's not about me. Not about my pride or even my feelings, it's about my little girl and all the things she deserves. I cry harder, and John reaches down and pulls on my arm until I stand. Then he wraps his big body around mine and lets me cry all over him. I'm thinking they didn't expect all of this drama during our first meet-and-greet.

After I regain my composure, I say, "Yes. I could use your help. I'll move to Cincinnati, but I'll only live in your home until I can find my own place. I don't want the expense of the hotel until I find something. I also don't want to take advantage of you, but I need what you're offering; more importantly, my little girl needs it. I wasn't kidding when I said I haven't found much kindness in people, so to be honest I'm terrified."

"All right then. This letter says you have to be out of here in seventy-two hours. I'll call my boys and have them up here tomorrow to help us. Give your notice at work. I'll handle the landlord. I'm going to run to the hardware store and get some packing supplies, and we'll start now so that by the time the boys get here tomorrow we can load up."

I'm stunned by the speed that he's ready to move. He walks back into my tiny kitchen before I can say anything, and I hear him talking on his phone. He's trying to be discreet, but I hear him say, "Call out. I don't give a damn. This is family, and they need us. I'll see you tomorrow morning before lunch. Boy...I love you. Now call your brother and tell him what I just told you. If he has questions, he can call me."

He disconnects, grabs his keys from the table, and kisses his wife on the way out the door.

John made me post a *For Sale* sign on my car and

said the landlord will let us leave it here until it sells. I'm skeptical about this, but I'm not about to argue. He says he'll get me a better car, a reliable one, once we get to Cincinnati. I had to buy that one for fifteen hundred dollars after my other one was totaled. It looks like a cheap car and handles like one, too. I've been nervous about having the baby in it but thought it was better than standing at the bus stop with her exposed to all the elements and the local riff-raff.

****

When Matt's brothers show up the next day bright and early, I'm a nervous wreck. Thank goodness the brothers arrive at the same time that Matt's parents get to my place, or it would have been even more awkward.

Matt's brother, Steve, is quiet around me at first. He's watching me like a hawk and it's so uncomfortable, but I just try to suck it up and ignore him. Mariah's a different story; she and Steve are an instant hit with one another. He seems to even carry on a conversation with her and the babbling baby noises she makes. The smile he gives her is one of genuine affection.

Johnny's different. He's quiet, pleasant, and helpful, but not overbearing. I catch him watching me, too, but it's different with him; it's like he's trying to figure me out. He also hit it off with Mariah right away.

Both brothers are handsome but look nothing alike. Steve is a carbon copy of Matt. It's disturbing at first, especially when I think of my last encounter with Matt. I keep getting freaked out when I see him out of the corner of my eye. I'm afraid I'll call him Matt by accident, that's how close the resemblance is. I think that's making me more tense than I already am. For the first hour, it was causing my belly to do flips, but the more he talks, the more the differences are apparent. Steve seems gentler, more laid back, where Matt always seemed to be bigger than any room he was in.

Johnny is taller and broader through the shoulders than both of his brothers. He's also a little more rugged, a blue-collar kind of man. It's obvious that Matt and Steve are the suit-and-tie guys. Johnny just seems a little less polished and a little more good ol' boy. His hair is the same brown as the other two, just a little longer, and his eyes are the same color as his mother's—an arresting, intense green. I find myself watching him more than I should. I'm drawn to him like no one ever before. There's something about him that I find calming. He's melt-your-panties-hot, but there's something else about him that I can't put my finger on. I'm also completely enchanted, because he's so different from his brothers.

So far, all of the Brownings are proving to be good with Mariah, and she seems to like all of them, too. I'm fascinated watching her interact with all three of the men, because up until now, the only man she's ever been exposed to is the pediatrician she sees during an exam.

It's obvious that John was an active participant in raising his kids. He doesn't bat an eyelash when Mariah spits up all over him and even takes over feeding her when the rest of us are busy packing and loading. Steve is tender and sweet with her. He treats her like a little princess, and she can't take her eyes off him when he's near.

Johnny's silly with her. He gives her raspberries on her plump little arms, neck, and belly while she squeals and giggles. When he holds her where she can reach his face, she yanks on his goatee causing him to chuckle every single time.

We finish loading the truck in about two hours, and since I'm leaving my car here in Indy, Mariah and I have to ride with one of them. Steve is driving the U-Haul, so that's out, and it looks like Judy packed a bunch of stuff in her car. I guess Mariah and I are riding in Johnny's extended cab truck. I wrestle the car seat into the back seat, locking it into place and load her in. I feel a sliver of fear as we pull out of the parking lot. It's not overwhelming enough for me to stop the car, but it's enough that I'm aware.

This whole situation is bizarre. I still can't believe any of this is happening. I can't believe I'm trusting people I don't even know to help take care of us. I wish I'd made different choices in my life up to this point, so I wasn't in a position to need to rely on strangers, but I didn't. So, here I am driving down the interstate, headed for a new life with a new family, in a car with a virtual stranger.

****

Johnny

I decide to cut to the chase and ask how she met Matt. I've never been good at bullshitting. I'm a right-to-the-point kind of guy. I've lain awake in bed every night trying to understand what my brother was thinking, having women on the side.

I almost wish I'd never have asked her though. My brother was a total douchebag. If what she's saying is true, then he really did a number on her. I can't believe he freaked out on her and left. I can't imagine what was going through her head when he walked away and never came back. If Matt were alive, I'd beat his ass. It's a hard thing to reconcile when the person you don't understand is dead and you can't confront them.

The sad thing is that Matt walking out on her isn't the worst part or the end of her shitty story. After everything she's already been through, she's now moving away from her home to be near a bunch of people she doesn't know just so her daughter will have a family. How fucked up is that? Either she has the worst luck of anyone on the planet, or she's an idiot. After talking with her, I don't think she's stupid, but who knows, only time will tell. No matter what angle you look at her story from, it's still talk show gold.

I do know that she's gorgeous; her long brown hair is so shiny it should be in a shampoo commercial. She has a petite, curvy body with shapely legs and a heart-shaped ass. Her skin is a creamy ivory that begs to be touched. The stunning, wide, emerald eyes so much like my own are the first thing I see when I look at her face, but she has perfect full lips and a small straight nose. There's the hint of a dimple in her left cheek. For some reason, I'm dying to make her smile so I can see how deep it really goes.

I tell her about Lisa coming to inform us about her and the baby, and how Lisa encouraged us to contact her. She seems surprised by this, but if she knew Lisa outside of this situation, she'd know that's just how she is. I also let her know that I had no idea what Matt was doing, but Steve suspected it and even confronted him about it.

"To be honest I'm fucking pissed at my brother, but I don't blame you for any of it. I'm pretty sure that no one blames you. Steve freaked out at first, because he's always been close with Lisa. He was actually in love with her in high school, and Matt stole her right out from under him. Damn, Steve was pissed. They broke Mom's glass coffee table fist fighting over it. I don't think they spoke for weeks. I know Steve was quiet today, but he'll warm up. It'll just take some time. He's mad at my brother right now for having you on the side and whoever else he was stringing along, too. The whole thing is just a mess."

"I'm a little nervous about running into Lisa," she confesses in a whisper. "I can tell that you all are still close to her, and I don't think it would go well if we end up in the same room. I'd be respectful, but I don't want to upset her any more than I already have. She's been good to me despite the circumstances. She was very generous with the offer for Matt's estate. My lawyer said she split it right down the middle and gave Mariah half. She even thought to give a portion to her for college and more as an adult. That's pretty amazing."

"No need to worry about that. She moved to Florida last week. She was down there interviewing for a job about the same time she was finding out the answer to the paternity test results. She'll be okay; she's a tough girl. You're right, though; we are still close to her, probably always will be. She's been part of our lives for almost twenty years. You don't just flush relationships like that with good people, but it won't affect anything with you either. We'll just plan our visits with her so your paths don't cross. It'll be okay."

I try to sound reassuring for her. There's something about this woman that makes me want to protect her and take care of her. I haven't felt that way before, and it surprises me. Maybe I'm more like my dad than I thought, just wanting to make things right after my brother left such a mess.

"I figured that she's pretty amazing. I don't understand why Matt pursued me when he had her. She's beautiful, educated, thoughtful, and was obviously in love with him. I'll never understand. If a girl like her gets cheated on, there was never any hope for someone like me. I feel horrible about all of it. If I'd known Matt was married, I never would have been with him, and if I found out prior to my visit to her house, I never would've gone there. That whole trip changed the path of my life and probably hers, too."

"What do you mean?"

"I lost my mind when I found out that Matt was dead. I passed out right on Lisa's doorstep. Then I passed out again when I found out that he was married. I was a mess. She was a mess. I got in the car and tried to drive back to Indy. That set the next chain of events in motion with the hospital and the bills. I never should have done that.

"I can't imagine what your parents must think of me. It's so embarrassing. This whole situation is something that you'd see in a TV movie. It's not something that happens to normal people."

"Unfortunately, you're living proof that this does happen to normal people. As for my dad, it's so damn obvious that he's trying to fix Matt's mistakes. He probably won't admit it, though. He loves his kids and is a fierce protector of all of us, but it broke his heart how bad Matt screwed up. He took it to heart and even apologized to Lisa, because he felt like he didn't raise Matt better."

"What? Seriously? It's not his fault. I'm not sure any of us will ever know why he did what he did. It's no one's fault, but Matt's."

"On the upside to all this, my dad's thrilled to have a grandbaby. My sister and her husband have been trying, but no luck yet, and Steve and his wife Mary aren't quite ready. So when he heard about Mariah, I'm surprised he didn't skip out the door that day and show up on your doorstep. You'll never find a more devoted family man than him.

"My mom has been an emotional basket case for the last year. Having to bury her son almost killed her. Then to find out what kind of man he really was…" I shake my head. "I thought we'd lose her for sure. The only bright spot has been your daughter. My mom was on cloud nine with that baby in her arms today. I'm surprised she didn't try to make you ride with her so she'd get more time with Mariah. Moving here won't just be good for you, it'll be good for all of us. You'll see."

"Well, I can never repay the kindness of your family. I'll sure try, though. I'll also do my best not to take advantage of their goodwill."

"You don't need to repay anything. Just allow us to be a part of Mariah's life, and that should cover things."

Chapter Three

Jill

We make small talk the rest of the ride there, and I find that I really like Johnny. He's a straight shooter with a kind heart. He's very much his father's son and so different from Matt. I can see little bits of Matt in all three of the men, but thank God no more than that. I'm still hurting from the way everything went down last year. I'm not sure I'll ever be the same or ever trust a man again, not fully.

Two weeks later, I'm moving into my own apartment about five miles from John and Judy. Apparently, John back paid my rent in Indy, and allowed the landlord to keep whatever money he made selling my car. Then John refused to let me pay him back so I was able to use the first check from Matt's estate that was retroactive to Mariah's birth, to get a small two-bedroom apartment in a clean complex in a decent part of town. I also found a job as an elementary school janitor in downtown Cincinnati. The work is kind of gross, and it means I'll have long days and a little bit of a commute, but it's the best I can do. I'm most excited because the school district offers medical and dental benefits after ninety days.

Our new schedule is a busy one. I drop Mariah off at six o'clock in the morning at daycare and one of the Brownings picks her up and takes her to their house, feeds her, sometimes bathes her, and then I pick her up and take her home.

Until my benefits with the school kick in, I have to purchase a temporary insurance policy for both of us. It's expensive, so I approached John and Judy once again and asked for more help. It's killing me to ask for help, but I need to do what's best for my girl and not what's best for my pride. The quickest way for me to make money is to waitress at a bar on the weekends. To do that, I have to have someone watch Mariah overnight on Friday and Saturday and schedule in time to see her during the day. I hate giving up all that time with her, but I just keep telling myself that it's a necessary evil and only short term. I only need to do this for three months until those benefits kick in.

John bought me a nice used car and refused to let me pay him anything for it. He said it made him feel better to know we weren't riding around in that old piece of shit I had before. My new car is a cute little Honda Civic that's only about four years old and was owned by an old woman from their church, so there were only about fifteen thousand miles on it. Johnny said he's been servicing that car since the lady bought it, so he knows it's in excellent condition.

I've never been more thankful for a person than I am for Lisa Browning. As strange as that is to say, if it weren't for her kindness, we'd be living on the streets with no hope of ever getting off of them. The sad part is, it makes me hate Matt even more. I can't believe he'd cheat on such an amazing woman. I don't know anyone as selfless as she is. Who does what she's done for Mariah under those circumstances, with the money *and* with the Brownings? I'm still floored and trying to find a way to thank her that might be appropriate. There's not really a Hallmark card that says thanks to my baby-daddy's wife for saving my life.

****

It's the Thursday after I move into my own place, and I've just gotten Mariah into the high chair when I hear a knock at the door. When I look through the peephole, I see Johnny. I wasn't expecting him, so I'm a little perplexed as to why he's here. I open the door.

"Hey, Johnny."

"Hi, Jill. I thought maybe you'd like some pizza tonight. I hope I caught you before you made dinner." His smile is bright as he holds up the pizza box.

"No. I mean yes. I mean no, I haven't eaten; yes, I'd like pizza. Come on in." I step aside so he can come in. He greets Mariah with a kiss on the cheek and gets busy doling out the pizza.

"I appreciate you bringing pizza over, but I have to ask, why?" I chew on the inside of my lip waiting for his response.

"You don't know anyone here, and you worked all day." He shrugs. "I just thought it might help."

My hearts thumps a little stronger listening to his words. "It does. I'm just not used to anyone thinking of me."

"Well, it's time you start expecting that sort of thing. If the people around you care, they're going to do things like this sometimes. Now, come on and eat. I can feed the baby."

I don't argue, I just thank him and dig in.

After dinner, we sit in the living room and talk for an hour before he excuses himself. For being a beast of a man, he has the most tender and thoughtful heart. I can't figure out why he's single; he's such a good catch. Once he's gone and I'm lying in my bed alone, I find myself thinking about what it would feel like to have strong arms like his wrapped around me. There's a feeling of safety in his presence that I've never felt with anyone, and I love when he's around.

****

It's been a month and a half since I moved to Cincinnati and although things are going well here, I'm lonely as hell. Johnny's been over three more times with pizza or Chinese food, and I've enjoyed those moments immensely, but I've only made one friend, Valerie, and I only see her on the weekends at the bar. I have the Brownings who are fantastic, but they are not my people. They have all taken to helping with Mariah, even Tara, Matt's sister who makes no secret of hating me. They all treat Mariah like a little angel and fight to watch her. Steve even bought his own car seat, and it has a permanent place in the backseat of his truck. John, Judy, and Johnny have been awesome to me, but it's not the same as having a friend or a boyfriend or even my own family. Some days I just want someone to talk to that cares about more than just my daughter or someone that doesn't babble and coo. It's better that I don't, though, because I have no idea where I'd find the time for a friend.

Even though I had no one in Indy, it didn't seem as lonely. Maybe it was because I wasn't surrounded by people who have close relationships with one another and enjoy being together. They try to include me, but I know they're just being nice, which makes me feel even more like an outsider. You'd think with my lack of time I wouldn't even notice, but I do. I notice every hug, every smile, every laugh, and every look they all share. Those are the things I've craved all of my life and have never found. I thought I had it with Matt, but it's obvious that was a farce. It's almost worse to think you have it and then have it jerked away.

My crazy schedule goes like this: I leave my house at five forty-five Monday through Thursday and don't get home until almost eight o'clock at night. Then I spend a few minutes with Mariah and put her to bed. On Friday, I work at the bar, so I leave my house at five forty-five for the school job and don't usually drag back through my door until two in the morning or later, after the bar job. Mariah stays with Steve or Tara on those nights. I pick her up at eight in the morning on Saturday and spend as much time with her as I can, because I don't see her more than a few minutes during the week. Then I drop her back off at six thirty in the evening on Saturday at Judy's. On Sunday, I don't pick her up until the late afternoon because I work the day shift. Then I have a few hours with her before she goes to bed.

It's a tough schedule to keep, and it's slowly killing me. I can see the dark circles under my eyes when I look in the mirror. I've lost some weight, and I'm afraid I'll end up sick, but I can't ask for any more help. I'm already blessed beyond reason with what I have.

It's the day before Thanksgiving, and I've been asked to work at the bar. They tell me it's the biggest bar night of the year, and after clearing it with Tara, I accept. I don't work at the school because of the holiday on Thursday and Friday.

I drop Mariah off with Tara's husband, because she and the rest of the family are at John and Judy's.

Apparently, Lisa is coming to town and has asked to see them this evening, so we all thought it would be better if the baby wasn't there. After I leave her house, I merge onto I-275 to go to work and, of course, since this is my life, something has to go wrong. I blow a tire. I pull off to the side of the road with a *thunk, thunk, thunk* as the flat, lopsided rubber rolls under my rim.

Groaning in frustration, I get out of the car and try to change it myself, but once I get the tire off and pull the spare out of the trunk I realize that my spare is flat. I have no way to fix this without help, and as much as I hate to ask for more of that, I have no choice. I remove my ancient cell phone from my purse and with frozen fingers dial the number to work to let them know I'll be late. My boss is sizzling with attitude and threatens to fire me, but I can't change the tire with a magician's wand, so he'll just have to wait.

The cars are speeding past me, thrusting the frigid air at me like the winds of a hurricane and it's already cold as hell out here. My body gives an involuntary shudder, so I climb back in my car and ponder a way out of this without calling the Brownings. It's at this point when something inside me cracks a little, and I realize just how helpless I am and how little I can take care of myself. I don't have AAA and a tow truck would defeat the purpose of working tonight because I'd just use my tips to pay for that and a taxi. The tears begin to fall. Not just a tear here or there, but big wet ones with snot and sobbing hiccups. Truth be told, I'm exhausted and feeling sorry for myself.

I calm myself down the best I can and do the only thing I know to do; I call Johnny. I'm most comfortable with him, and he's a mechanic. Actually, he owns his own shop, but he still does some of the work, and I know he could help me quickly and get me back on the road with little effort. I just hate to call because he's supposed to be seeing Lisa right about now.

Johnny answers on the second ring.

"Jill? Are you okay?" Concern is evident in his voice. He doesn't even say hello.

"Yes, well, no." I sniffle louder than I mean to. "I have a flat. I can usually change a tire, but the spare is flat. I'm sorry; I know Lisa will be there soon. I can change it once the spare is pumped up. I'm already late for work, and my boss is threatening to fire me."

He's quiet a moment before he asks, "Where are you?" The grumble of his voice is deeper than usual, and I can tell I've upset him.

"Southbound on I-275 past the Beechmont exit."

"You're going to change a tire on the side of the interstate in the dark? No fucking way! I'll be there in about ten minutes. Stay in your car and lock the doors. *Do not* open up for anyone but me. Got it?" Irritation drips from his voice as he barks out orders.

"I got it, but I'll be okay. I just need help with the spare. I don't want you to miss your company."

"Goddammit, woman. Don't argue with me. I'll be there soon. Do what I've told you to do." His command is harsh and has me cowering a little.

"Okay, Johnny. Thank you," I say, keeping my voice quiet, hoping to calm him down.

As he's hanging up, I can hear him fussing. I feel awful about it. I know he's mad at me, and that just makes me cry again. I swear my life is never going to get better. Always imposing on other people, asking for too much. Living paycheck to paycheck. I just don't see an end in sight.

It's not a full ten minutes later when Johnny is standing by the door to my car tapping on the window, a scowl on his handsome face.

"Grab your purse and give me your keys," he demands. There are no pleasantries, just orders from an irritated man.

"Why? I just need you to pump up the spare so I can get to work and worry about the rest later."

"You're not riding on a pumped up spare tire. My tow truck guy is going to come get it and take it to the shop. I'll get you a regular tire, a new spare, and take your car to work. For now, I'm going to drive you there, so grab your stuff."

"I can't ask you to do all of that. It's a holiday, and you have company visiting."

"Don't argue with me. Just get in my truck and give me your keys. I'm going to handle this, and I don't want a bunch of lip about it." His tone brooks no argument, so I grab my stuff, yank my coat tight around my body, and make my way to his truck.

It's freaking cold, and I have a headache from crying so much. The guilt about taking him away from his family tonight is weighing me down, and I just want to go home, but I have to work. I have two more months of these crazy hours. I can survive that. Or that's what I keep telling myself.

Two hours after he drops me off at the bar, he returns and gives me my keys without a word. Instead of leaving, he sits down at the bar and buys a drink. What in the hell is he doing? He's supposed to be seeing Lisa. I don't want his whole family to think I'm trying to keep him from her. He hasn't said a word to me. He just watches me hustle around the room.

Even pissed off, he's hot. Not your polished suit-and-tie kind of sexy. He's the rough hands, five o'clock shadow, body ripped with muscles from blue-collar work kind of hot. Sometimes when I see him right after work, I can still smell the auto shop on him, and it does funny things to my libido. I think if he weren't Matt's brother, I'd have launched myself at him by now. While he sits there at the bar, looking all broody, it does nothing but amp the heat up between my legs more. Why is it that I'm ready to drag him to a supply closet and rip his clothes off when he's so pissed at me and won't look me in the eye? I must be a complete idiot.

I feel like I'm doing something wrong every time I steal a glance at him, but I just can't seem to help myself. If it weren't so busy in here, I'd be having full, detailed fantasies about him while I work.

Close to eleven o'clock, the crowd gets thicker and rowdier. The guys are more than halfway drunk, and of course when it's like this, they tend to get touchy-feely. It's my least favorite part of working at a bar. I step up to get drink orders from a loud group of college age guys in the corner when one of them grabs me and pins me to the wall, knocking my serving tray to the floor.

"Let me go, Asshole!" I yell at him over the music as I squirm to get away from him.

A sliver of panic crawls over me when he laughs at my request. He's too drunk to care that I'm not into this. This guy reeks of cheap booze and cigarettes, and I'm freaking out. The bouncers are either by the dance floor or by the entrance, and there is no one to help me. No one in his group is even paying attention to what's going on. I panic enough that I kick up and catch him in the nuts. Instead of falling to the ground like they do in the movies, he bends forward a little and cracks my cheek with a backhand powerful enough to drop me to the ground in a heap. The force of the blow is so hard it feels like a frying pan hit my face.

College boy is still standing in front of me complaining about the kick I gave him while I'm on my knees trying to clear my eyes and figure out how to get out of this situation. Before I can do anything, he's yanked from in front of me, and I jump to my feet hoping to scramble away while I have the chance. I'm startled to realize that Johnny is wailing on this guy with his fists.

It doesn't take even a minute for the bouncers to be there breaking it up. They're dragging Johnny to the door along with the asshole that hit me. I run after the bouncer who has Johnny and yell at him that Johnny was just trying to help me. He ignores me and continues pushing his way through the crowd. We get all the way outside when the bouncer turns to me and says, "If you fight in our club, you get kicked out. It doesn't matter the reason. He's got to go."

Johnny spins on him and gets in his face.

"That guy hit her. He pinned her against the wall, and when she fought back, he backhanded her and there was no one there to take care of her. I wasn't just going to let that go. Someone has to look out for her."

Johnny is breathing fire, he's so furious.

"Man, it's packed in there. We're doing the best we can. Now go on home. She'll be fine. That guy is out of there now, so no more worries."

The bouncer turns on his heel to stalk away.

"Fuck that, man. If I'm not in there, who is going

to keep an eye on her? Are you too busy to keep your fucking servers safe?"

"No, it's just a busy night. Shit happens. She'll get over it and go back to do her job."

That's the wrong thing for the bouncer to say because Johnny turns to me and orders, "Get your shit, Jill. You're not staying somewhere you aren't safe. And this fuckwad can't guarantee that you will be. Let's go."

His tone leaves no room for argument, but I still have bills to pay so I argue anyway.

"Johnny, I can't quit. I've got extra bills to pay at least for a few more months. It'll be okay. I'm sure I'll be fine the rest of the night."

"No, it fucking won't. Grab your shit and let's go. Let me worry about the bills. It's not good for your daughter if you end up in the hospital because some douchebag put his hands on you. Now get your shit and get to the car."

He's flaming mad. Scary mad. It's similar to the day that Matt left me, but the anger is not directed at me, it's directed at the guy who hit me and the bouncer that couldn't keep me safe. The fury in his eyes is frightening, but in the end, I do what he says because he's right. He's not trying to scare me; he's trying to help me. I'll look for another job starting Friday.

"Okay, Johnny. Let me get my stuff and tell the manager."

"I'll wait right here. If you aren't out of there in five minutes, I'm coming in for you."

"Okay. I'll be right back."

Five minutes later, I'm back in my car and headed to Tara's to get Mariah. I'd said goodbye to Johnny, but he just grunted at me. When I pull up to Tara's house the lights are out, so I turn around and head home. I hadn't realized how late it was until I pulled in her driveway. Tears roll down my cheeks the whole way home. I shouldn't have any left the way I've sobbed all day, but it seems that I haven't cried myself out all the way. When I pull into my complex, I notice that Johnny's truck is parked right next to my normal spot. Shit. Is he here to yell at me now? I don't think I can take anything else happening tonight.

I get out of my car and swipe at my eyes. Johnny gets out and follows behind me without a word. I open the door and let him follow me in. I don't say anything because I'm not sure what to say. With my back to him, I set my purse down on the table and close my eyes. I wait for the yelling to start. It doesn't happen.

Instead, his hand grabs my arm turning me around to face him. With one look at my face, his eyes soften. He pulls me into his big, strong arms, and I fall apart again, sobbing and shaking while he holds me. Eventually, he carries me over to the couch, sits down, and nestles me into his lap. Then he wraps his arms back around me and pushes my head to his chest. I'm sure I look like a little kid in his lap, crying into his shirt, but I don't care. I'm just thankful to have someone hold me. So damn thankful. It's been too long.

His hand brushes over my hair with tender strokes until I finally settle down, and the only sounds left are the hiccup at the end of a sob-fest and my sniffles. The rhythm of his hands and the rise and fall of his chest are soothing me like nothing has in a very long time.

"I'm sorry about the job, Jill, but they couldn't keep you safe. When I saw that guy pin you to the wall,

I started trying to get to you. I was still a few people away when he hit you, and I swear to God I couldn't think of anything better than killing him."

"Thanks for helping me. I can find another job. I'm just so tired of barely getting by. I work so hard. I'm so damn tired all the time, but I try not to think about that. Instead, I try to focus on how lucky I am to have Mariah and all of you to help. Then I feel guilty about having to rely on you all. I know Tara hates me, and Steve isn't much better. If I could find another way, I swear I would. My life is such a damn mess. It always has been, though. The best days of my life were with Matt. I've never had anyone treat me that good. What I got from him at the end was just par for the course. My parents even hate me. As a mother, I have no idea how in the world you can hate your kid. I'd do absolutely anything for my girl."

"God, how could someone as sweet as you get dealt such a shitty hand in life? I fucking hate my brother for what he did to you. He was such an asshole, and I can't even tell him that. I was envious of him for years. He had a great job where he made a ridiculous amount of money, had a nice house, and an awesome wife, only to find out that he was a fraud and a user."

I have nothing to say to that, because it's the honest to God truth. We stay quiet for a long time, and I know I should let him go, but I'm feeling selfish and can't end it before he does. At some point, I must doze off because I feel myself being lifted. I blink my eyes open and realize it's Johnny carrying me, so I turn my head into his shirt and take a deep breath through my nose. I'm trying to soak up the light mix of auto shop and cologne that's all Johnny; it's a manly scent I now crave. I almost want to roll around on him like a dog in the grass, so I can have it all over my clothes for the rest of the night.

Gently, he sets me on my feet and brushes the hair over my shoulders, following the movement of his hands with his eyes. Then he steps closer, so much closer that I get the hint of beer on his breath from the bar. My knees go a little weak, and I hope that I don't embarrass myself by falling in front of him. His big, calloused hands shift from my neck to my jaw where he holds my face reverently as he stares into my eyes.

His emerald greens shine with lust and need, and by the way my core is heating, I'm certain he can see the same in mine. He leans in and places his lips on mine, softly, sweetly, closed at first. Our mouths fit so perfectly together. Then I slide my arms around his neck and open up for him, desire pulling me in. He gives a low groan, and licks my lower lip before sliding his tongue into my mouth.

Our tongues tangle in a passionate dance of perfect synchronicity, like we've been doing this together forever. My hands explore the ridges and dips of his chest as he grips my ass and lifts, holding us pelvis to pelvis. My legs automatically wrap around his waist, and there's no doubt what he wants from me in that moment. I shift my hips so that his rock hard cock hits the perfect spot at my center. I moan into our kiss and roll my hips this time working on getting the perfect level of friction through our clothes. He takes two, long steps, and traps me against the wall so I can't move. My body is on fire; I'm so hot for him and what he's willing to give me. God, I've dreamt about this moment a hundred times since he walked into my apartment in

Indiana, and I'm having a hard time remembering why this wasn't a good idea.

Gripping the bottom of my blouse, he tugs upward until I'm free of it. His large hand slides up my bare torso tugging the cup of my bra down so he can access the sensitive point beneath the fabric. The first pass his thumb makes over it robs me of my breath, and I do my best to arch my back, pushing more of me into his hand. I can feel his smile against my lips right before he pinches the tight bud between his pointer finger and thumb. Lightning zings straight to my clit and I cry out. The sensation is so strong and the feeling is so good that I moan again, begging for more. I'm almost delirious as his hand shifts to the other breast, moving the cup a little more roughly before he pinches again. He shifts his mouth from mine to suck my nipple hard into his mouth while his tongue twirls inside. My head thumps against the drywall as I throw it back while my eyes squeeze shut. "Johnny!"

I open my eyes, and with his head bent worshiping my engorged breasts, I'm able to really look around the room for the first time. What I see is like a cold bucket of water tossed over my head. Mariah's toys lay all over the house. Her blanket is tossed over the side of the couch, and a pack of new diapers sits on the table. It's then that I realize what I'm really doing and with whom I'm doing it. He must feel the change in my body language, the instant switch from hot to cold, because he lifts his head to look me in the eyes. It only takes a second or two before he lowers me to my feet and holds me tight against his chest, in a hug I've been craving for months.

I can feel the wild thrumming of his heart in his

chest as he fights for control of his body. The lust-fog was cleared for me the minute I realized I was about to have sex with Matt's brother. It doesn't matter that Matt was a jerk and now dead, it only matters that things would never work out for us and then it would be awkward for everyone.

With a heavy layer of regret blanketing my heart I tell him, "We shouldn't have done that."

He searches my face with wary eyes. "Why? We aren't doing anything wrong."

"I don't need to make things any more complicated with your family than they already are."

His arms drop to his sides and he steps back.

"What do you mean?" His confusion is obvious.

I lean over, snatch my shirt off the floor, and slide it back over my head as I answer. "You're the brother of my dead baby-daddy. Your family is helping me to survive and raise Mariah. Your sister and brother already hate me. Your parents would freak out. I can't imagine how much more that would be amplified if they got wind of what just happened. I can't risk losing the only real family life for my child that she'll ever know over lust. The price is too high."

"You think I'd do anything that would hurt you or Mariah? Do you think I'd risk hurting you both to satisfy a lusty urge?" He sounds a little angry.

"Not purposely, no. I'm just not in a position where I can risk it. I like you a lot, more than I should. I enjoy your company, and I think you're sexy as hell. I appreciate all that you do for me and my daughter, but I can't let it go any farther."

He takes two more steps back. The heat of his body is completely gone from mine now, and I miss it already. I can see the hurt flash in his eyes right before he turns for the door.

"I'm sorry you feel that way. I thought there was more to it with us, but if I'm only here to help out sometimes, I guess that's what I'll do. You're right; I never should have kissed you, but not for the reasons you gave me. I actually give a shit about you, and you obviously don't feel the same. That wasn't a spur of the moment kiss. Nothing that just happened was an impulsive mistake. I've been dreaming of that since the first day I met you. If you decide to get your head out of your ass, let me know. I'll see you at Mom's tomorrow."

I clench my eyes closed, cringing at his words. The only sound I hear is his boots clumping his retreat through the entranceway to the door. The smell of him has dissipated, and I'm standing here stunned. I don't even have a chance to respond, he's gone so fast. I'm not sure what to make of any of that.

Does he really feel that way? He wasn't looking for a one-night stand? Oh God, I'm seriously unequipped to make good judgment calls. It seems like my life is a series of mistakes that I can't escape. I bolt for the door, throwing it open as I sprint to the parking lot.

"Johnny! Johnny!" I scream.

He's almost to his truck by the time he turns back to me.

"Wait, Johnny. Don't leave mad. Please." I plead with him.

His expression is stormy under the parking lot lights, and I hate that I'm responsible for that.

"Johnny, I'm sorry. Please understand. I want you in more ways than I should, but it's not what's best for my daughter. If it didn't work out with us, things would be worse for me than they already are. Your family—"

He cuts me off. "Don't bring my family into this. They don't get a say in who I date or who shares my bed. I love them, but this isn't about them. It's about you and me." He punctuates that by pointing at me and then at himself.

"If you don't feel anything for me then just say it. If you do, stop wasting our time and let nature takes its course. What's it going to be, Jill?"

"I want you. I want there to be an us, but it's not the right thing. You've got to know that. I'm your brother's ex, the woman he cheated with. That's messed up, Johnny. It'll never be okay for us to be together."

His eyes and face lower to look at the asphalt. He shakes his head, and I'm wondering what he'll say next. He doesn't speak; he swiftly moves into my space and cups my jaw with his large hands as tenderly as possible. Then he kisses me. It's deep, it's hard, and it's full of meaning. Unfortunately, the meaning is goodbye. He separates from me and backs away.

"I think you're wrong, Jill, but if you don't want me, I won't beg. Just know that what we have between us doesn't come along very often, and you're throwing away something special. Goodbye, Jill."

"Johnny?"

He stops and waits, but never turns around. His hands are fisted in irritation, and his shoulders are tense. I don't know what to say so I stand there, freezing my butt off in the parking lot, wishing I were someone different, someone who deserves Johnny Browning and would be free to love him without issue. He tires of waiting for me to speak, so he gets in his truck and drives away, taking my heart with him.

****

It's hours before I fall asleep, so when my alarm sounds, I curse it as I smack it to turn off and get up. After I shower and get ready, I head to Johnny's hoping to catch him before he goes to his mom's for Thanksgiving dinner.

I arrive at his house and realize that his truck isn't in the driveway, but it could be in the garage, so I climb the couple of steps to reach his front door and knock. After a couple of minutes, I realize he's not home, so I turn to leave. Standing on the other side of the fence is a gorgeous woman, who looks to be around my age, and she's watching me. Her raven hair is cut into a sleek bob. She's in a short dress with stockings and knee high, kick-ass black boots.

"Are you looking for Johnny?"

"Yes, have you seen him?"

"Yeah, he left a couple of hours ago when my husband and I were coming back from our morning run. He was in a foul mood, so it's probably good you missed him."

"I'm certain that foul mood is my fault. I was trying to come apologize before I encounter that mood at his parents' house. Nothing like attitude at a holiday dinner table." I huff out an uncomfortable laugh.

"You must be Jill." She smiles brightly at me.

"Yes, should I ask how you know that?"

"Don't worry. I'm not judging, but just so you know, my parents are friends with John and Judy, so I know your story. Or at least the way they tell it. Our parents have been best friends since we were kids. I grew up down the street from them."

"Great." I'm sure the frustration is evident in my voice. I shift nervously as I suddenly wonder how many people know "my story."

"My name's Cici Hannigan. Short for Cecilia, but if you call me that, I may have to egg your car. As a kid, my mom sang that damn song to me so much I wanted to tape her mouth shut. Cecilia sounds too fancy anyway; I'm definitely a Cici. It's nice to finally meet you. John and Judy have had a lot of nice things to say, and your daughter is adorable. I saw her when she was with Johnny one day. That man is gone over her and so sweet with her. I'm not used to seeing him like that; it's nice."

"I'm surprised you've heard good things considering how we came to be a part of their lives."

"That's not your fault, or at least that's what John says. Also, I knew Matt for years, the *real* Matt. So it doesn't surprise me one bit. He was a douchebag in a sexy suit."

A dark look crosses her features, but she clears it just as fast as it came on.

"Can I ask what happened to your face?"

Groaning, I answer, "I worked at a bar until last night; one of the customers got a little too rowdy."

"That's pretty bad. Did you press charges?"

"No, I don't need any more issues. Besides, Johnny took care of that guy."

"Hey, some of my girlfriends and I go out about once a month for a girls' night out. Wanna join us? I'm not sure when the next one will be, but I'll call when I know."

"It depends on my job situation. Even though I quit the bar last night, I'm looking for a different weekend job now."

"I'll get your number from Johnny and give you a call. It was nice to meet you."

"Nice to meet you, too, Cici."

I climb in my car and head for the Browning home. Cici seems really nice. God, it would be so nice to have girlfriends again. It's been since high school that I've had anyone I was close with. My parents effectively scared them off as we got older.

****

Johnny

I can't believe Jill spewed all of that bullshit at me. It's almost like she thought I was only there to fuck her and then move on like nothing happened. I know her situation with my family is complicated. I also know they'd flip out if they knew how I feel about her, but I'm a grown man. I don't need their permission for this shit, and neither does she. They aren't going to cut her or Mariah out of their lives because they disapprove of our relationship.

Maybe I misread the cues. I don't usually have that problem. Women tend to be obvious about what they want even when they don't say it out loud. I thought she was into me, thought I'd sensed that for a couple of weeks now. Fuck. If she doesn't want me, then I'll be sure to keep my distance. Well, as much as I can. It's going to be difficult tomorrow since we're all getting together for the holiday, but after that I can make myself scarce.

The next morning, I'm exhausted and irritated. It takes me a two-hour workout to settle down enough to show up for the family dinner. I'm not quite ready to face Jill. Like a moth to a flame I'm drawn to her like no one ever before, and it pisses me off that she won't even consider me an option. I already bit Cici's head off this morning in the front yard for no reason. I owe her and Denton an apology, but that will have to wait until I've calmed down.

I try to think of anything other than that hot little encounter with her last night and the words that followed as I walk into my parent's house. Bobby's car is in the driveway, but I don't think anyone else is here yet.

Tara's in the kitchen helping Mom, and Bobby is on the floor playing with Mariah. As soon as that baby sees me, she lifts her chunky little arms up in a come-get-me motion and gives me the biggest damn grin. This kid is too cute. I've fallen for her as fast and as hard as her mother. I sweep her up into my arms and tickle her little belly. She giggles like crazy and yanks at my goatee in between smacks on my cheek. That's our thing, and I secretly love it.

I walk into the kitchen to say hi to the ladies and kiss them both on the cheek.

My sister appears a little tired so I ask, "You okay, Sis?"

She sighs.

"Yeah, yeah. I'm okay. Just tired. Mariah was up a lot last night. She must be teething because she wouldn't settle. It's unlike her, but I'm okay. I'll get a nap after we eat. I just hope she sleeps tonight. I can't do another night like last night."

"You don't have to worry about that. Jillian quit her job last night. She'll look for another one I'm sure, but some guy tried to grope her and when she resisted, he backhanded her. I saw the whole thing. I ended up kicking the guy's ass and got thrown out. When she followed me, the bouncer said he was too busy to keep an eye on everyone, meaning he didn't give a shit. Jill was ready to walk back in the door for the paycheck, but I told her no way and made her go home."

Both my mom and sister are staring at me like I've lost my mind.

"What? You think I should've let her go back in there? No freakin' way. It was too dangerous."

"She listened to you?" my mom inquires.

"Yeah, I told her it wouldn't be the best idea for Mariah to see her all beat up if someone acted like that again and a bouncer wasn't around to help her. It's one thing to work in a place like that when the bouncers keep the ladies safe, but when they don't care? Not worth it. She has to think about the baby now."

Mom watches me with a thoughtful expression for a minute and then goes back to her task.

Tara says in her snottiest tone, "Well, whatever, at least I'll get some sleep tonight. She can finally watch her own kid. I feel like I'm being used."

Whoa! What the hell? That came out of nowhere.

About that time, we hear the rustle of a bag and the thump of something heavy hit the floor behind us. Jill stands in the doorway with a huge black and blue mark across her cheek and a shocked expression, like she's been slapped. I have no idea what she's heard or what she thinks was said, but I can tell by the look on her face it's not good. After our conversation last night, I'm not sure what to do.

The hurt on her face is so apparent it pains me to look at her. The room is dead silent for a whole minute, and no one moves or says a word until she finally speaks up. Her voice shakes like she's barely holding on. I want to go to her, to comfort her or something. I want to do anything to get that look off her face, but I don't. I stand frozen, partially because of our words from last night and partially in fear.

"Tara, if watching my kid is too much for you, why didn't you say something? I would've figured something else out. I thought you wanted to do it. I never meant to push her on you."

Jill's eyes fill with tears, and I notice that her empty hands are trembling with emotion. My sister spins around to her and with more venom than I thought possible, blurts out, "Of course you didn't, but my parents are too old to be staying up all night with a screaming kid. I take her so they don't have to. My brothers say they will but so far haven't done it willingly. There's no one left. I'm not going to leave my niece to fend for herself, since you have better things to do."

I can tell Jill is close to losing it. Quietly, and I'm talking the spooky quietly where you know someone is about to unleash hell on your ass, Jill squares her shoulders and says, "Tara, first of all, I would never leave my infant to *fend for herself*. I don't know why you'd think I would. That tells me everything about what you think of me. Second, you will no longer be bothered with my *screaming kid*. In fact, I won't push her on any of you anymore. I had no idea you all felt that way. I thought you wanted her. I knew you didn't want me, would rather I disappear, but not her. This was her only shot at a real family. My family hates me as much as you do. I'm so damn sorry I did this to all of you. I should never have come here; I just wish I'd heard this long before today."

Her eyes are swimming with tears. She strides over and carefully takes Mariah from my arms placing a sweet kiss on her little head.

"Jill." I mutter her name, emotion thick in my voice. I know she's hurting, and I hate it.

I want her to look at me, to know that I don't feel the way that my sister does, that none of us do, but she won't. The tears are running like a river down her beautiful face. Mariah reaches back for me, but Jill holds her close and walks back out the door without another word. I follow her through the kitchen door and watch with a deepening sadness as she grabs her purse and the diaper bag from the couch as she leaves.

I wish I could've stopped her, but I have no idea what words to use. My sister was hateful, and I'm not sure what I could say to make things better. I march back into the kitchen pissed as hell ready to face off with Tara.

"Tara!" I hear my mom admonish as she cries.

Tara won't look at her. She just cusses and slams pots all around. Bobby and my dad rush into the room as I lose it.

"What the fuck, Tara? Seriously? What was that all about? I said a million times I'd take that baby overnight, but you always insisted. You acted like having her with you was the best thing in the world. Now you're acting like there's nothing worse. Are you fucking kidding me? Jill already thinks you hate her. Why would you do that?"

Tara turns furious eyes on me.

"I do hate her! She's using us, goddamn it! She's taken over our lives. We had to rearrange everything last night so Lisa could visit without it being an issue. Bobby had to miss being here just so Jill could go to work and have someone else take responsibility for her kid. Then she had to drag you away, too, to fix her car. When she was playing the other woman, she should've realized that she might get stuck holding the bag. That's what happens when you spread your legs for anyone, taking what isn't yours to begin with."

My mother gasps and slaps her hand over her own mouth. My dad just continues to glare at all of us, pissed off. He doesn't say a word; it's almost like he's just waiting for us to drop all of the dirt before he wades in.

"And don't forget that she fucking killed our brother!" Tara screeches.

I grip the edge of the island and lean across to where she stands. If I could breathe fire, there is no doubt I would right now.

"Tara, shut the hell up. That's not true. Matt was a...*fucking*...*cheater*! Jill wasn't the only one he was with. There were three others at the exact same time as her, and she didn't know it. She thought she was his one and only. It's not Jill's fault that he juggled several women at the same time, finally got one pregnant, and then stressed out so bad he had a heart attack. Jill thought they were starting a family together. So his reaction to her news was not her fault. He was the one who was married and lied to his wife. He's the one who used her and promised her everything he knew he'd never deliver on.

"Your perfect fucking Matt was a disgrace to our family and to husbands everywhere. It's screwed up that you'd stand there and blame Jill for everything. She has been nothing but nice to all of us. She knows you and Steve don't like her, but she puts up with the dirty looks and whispers behind her back so that her kid can have a relationship with us. Would you do that? No. Fucking. Way. Instead of helping her to make the best of this jacked up situation, you're tearing her down. I'm ashamed to call you my sister right now."

At the end of my last statement, my dad finally blows his top. "Enough!" He yells and slams his hands down on the counter with a bang causing everyone to jump. His face is as red as a tomato. His eyes are hard, and I can tell he's more pissed than he has ever been. Bobby is still in the doorway a few steps behind him and has not moved to Tara's side. Steve and Mary have arrived and are standing behind Bobby with perplexed looks on their faces. Mom is standing with her head down sobbing, as my dad makes his way across the room to her. He pulls her into his arms and whispers in her ear.

I turn to leave the room, and my dad growls, "Not another damn step, son. No one moves, no one leaves this room until you hear what I have to say."

I freeze. My dad hasn't made a demand like that since Matt, Steve, and I broke a bunch of windows in the neighbor's house when we were teenagers.

We all wait in uncomfortable silence until he gets my mom calmed down. Steve and Mary have moved into the room, but Bobby is still lingering by the door as he watches with wide eyes while this whole thing plays out. My dad turns so he can face us while still holding onto my mom who hasn't stopped crying.

"First of all," he points his finger at my sister, "Tara, if you didn't want to watch the baby, you should have said so. Your mother and I raised four kids and had no problem sharing baby duty in the middle of the night. We have a system we developed many years ago. We may be a little tired in the morning, but it's nothing we can't handle. We thought you'd like having a baby in the house and knowing how you idolized Matt, we thought it would be good for you to spend the time with her.

"Now that we know you don't feel that way, we'll be sure to keep you out of the loop. I can't and won't force her on you. She's a baby, a happy baby, and I want to keep it that way. If she senses your negative feelings toward her, she'll lose her little happy.

"As for the things you said about Jill and Matt, you're wrong." Dad's face is stone cold serious. "Matt lied to her and lied to several other women, too. I decided to talk to them. I was curious. Turns out they all got the same story. He traveled for work and just wanted to take things slow. In each town, he had a different one. Jill was the only one who happened to get pregnant. They all loved him, thought he was it for them. Those were some of the worst conversations of my life, but I had to know. I'm sure there were girls even before that, but I decided to stop digging up information.

"Tara, I don't have a clue about what's going on with your marriage, but I'm thinking that your issues aren't with Jill, they're with your own husband. Work them out. Don't bring that shit here and shovel it on everyone else. I love you, your mother loves you, your brothers love you, but you're a grown woman. Stop acting like a spoiled twelve year old. If you need to talk, just say something. We will be glad to listen to you. Don't treat other people like punching bags. It's not how you were raised."

He turns to Steve next.

"I don't know what your issue is either. Maybe you feel some kind of loyalty to Lisa, and I get that. I love Lisa like my own daughter, probably always will. I would do anything for her, but there is nothing to protect her from anymore. She's had to face it all. She wants us to have a relationship with Mariah and Jill. Hell, she gave us Jill's contact information. She gets the bigger picture here. She doesn't expect any of us to shun Jill for her. You need to get over your shit, but if you can't make that happen, then make yourself scarce when she's here. I won't tolerate anyone treating her that way under my roof when she has been through so much already. She got enough shit from your brother to last a lifetime, and I plan to spend the rest of my life making up for that."

He rotates his torso toward me and drills me with his eyes.

"Johnny, I realize you've gone and fallen for that girl."

There's an audible gasp from all the women in the room. Bobby is bug-eyed, and Steve looks pissed.

"I understand that. She's sweet, she works hard, she's good looking, she's a great mamma, and she adores you. Appreciates every little thing you do, but she is an emotional mess trying to find her place in this family and in the world. She has to find that on her own. You can't force it. Even if you make her yours, it won't automatically get her acceptance. Everyone has to accept her for who she is in their own time. I'm glad you want to protect her. Hell, I do, too, but there are some things we just can't protect her from. I'm not going to pass judgment on you for falling in love. It's the way of the world. It doesn't matter that she was Matt's first. He never respected her, and I'm not sure he ever loved her, so he didn't deserve her.

"But the bottom line is this—and everyone listen closely." He looks around the room making eye contact with everyone as he goes. "Matt. Is. Dead." He punctuates every word with his pointer finger into the counter like he's physically placing periods. "He's not coming back. He was my son, and I love him still, but I've never been more ashamed in my life than I am of who he turned out to be. I don't care that he had a nice house, a college degree, and a good job. He was *not* a good man. He used women and cheated on all of them and to be honest, they were all wonderful women, and those are just the ones we know about."

He turns back to me and says a little more calmly.

"If you care about Jillian and you think you can love her like she deserves, then go for it. Your mother and I will support you. But don't go after her unless you have ideas for the long run. She's not the kind of girl you date for a couple of months and walk away from.

"Now, the last thing I'm going to say is this. I don't *ever* want to hear again that Jill killed Matt. Matt killed himself. He put all the stress on himself by juggling different women and having unprotected sex. Once the shit hit the fan, he knew he was losing control, and the stress is what got him. It's not scientifically proven, but that's the only reason a healthy thirty-two-year-old man has a massive heart attack. Stress."

My dad walks over to my sister who is looking at the floor with tears in her eyes, arms crossed tight against her chest. He places his hands on her shoulders, and she looks up at him.

"Honey, Jill didn't kill Matt. Matt killed Matt. I love you, but your anger is misplaced. Let it go. Try to be reasonable. It's okay to realize you loved and idolized a flawed man. We all did. We just have to accept that and move on. Stop putting the blame where it doesn't belong. Okay?"

She nods and then falls into my dad's arms sobbing.

Bobby strides toward her and takes her from my dad.

I hear Bobby tell her in a quiet voice, "I'd never do to you what Matt did. I promise. Never. I love you, and I know you deserve better than that. You have to start trusting me again. Don't lump me in with Matt. Not every man is like him."

He leads her out of the room. Steve asks what happened, and I give him the CliffsNotes version.

"Shit." Steve grunts out. "I do like her. I stopped blaming her pretty quickly but just didn't know how to make things better. I love Mariah. I don't want her to think I don't. Mary and I would do anything for either one of them. I think we should go get them and bring them back."

I shake my head as I respond, "I don't know if that's a good idea. Tara isn't ready for that, and we don't want to make things worse. I'll try to go by today after dinner. Maybe you could stop by tomorrow to see her and tell her how you feel. She needs to hear it from you. She thinks you hate her, and Tara's words only made that seem more true. I'm going to try to call her now. I need to make sure she's okay."

I step out of the room and dial her number.

****

Jill

I've just put Mariah down for a nap when I hear my phone ring. I check the caller I.D. and see that it's Johnny. I can't pick it up now. Today's scene is what I've been trying to avoid. I just thought Mariah made things different. I thought she'd be able to have the family life I've never had, even if I was sort of on the sidelines of that family. Turns out that her affiliation to me is what will keep her from having that. It breaks my heart. There is nothing worse in this world than feeling unloved. I've decided it's the quickest way to crush a soul.

Today's fight brought some more issues to the forefront. I no longer have help with daycare pick-up or weekend sitters. I'm not quite sure how I'm going to do it. I may have to look into an apartment downtown near my job. The neighborhood is a scary kind of horrible, but I won't be able to make it to pick her up by six when the daycare closes if I keep my job and she stays where she is. My life is always one step forward, ten back.

I decide that I'll go to the library tomorrow to use their computer and look for different apartments, different daycare places, and different jobs. Something has to work out. For now, I'll just rest while the baby does. When she wakes up, I'll put her in the stroller and take her for a stroll. I can't look at these four walls the rest of the day and night. My television broke a few months after Matt left, and I never had the money to replace it. I don't have any books in the house because I never have time to read, so I have nothing to do.

I lie down on the couch and try to relax, but end up thinking of the last couple of years of my life and crying until I can't see straight. I must have dozed off, because I wake up to the muffled sound of Mariah fussing. I go get her out of her crib, change her diaper, and bundle her up. Then I put her in the stroller, and we take a very long walk. It's surprising, but she's happy to be outside, babbling her baby sounds as we go. Even though it's November, the sun is out and white puffy clouds fill the sky. It's a lovely, but chilly day.

When we get back to the apartment, I fix a peanut butter and jelly sandwich and feed Mariah. Then I bathe her, read to her, and put her to sleep. As I lie in bed, I think about Johnny and wonder if he'll ever speak to me again. I screwed up last night, but it turns out I was right. If Tara hates me now, I can't imagine how she'd feel if she found out I was seeing Johnny. I just can't take any more drama, but I am going to miss him, everything about him. He's been such a bright spot in all of this for me.

****

Over the weekend, I get a newspaper and scour it for jobs. I circle several waitress jobs and figure I need to find a babysitter I can pay to watch the baby while I work those hours. Paying a sitter will seriously cut into the money I'm making for insurance and other bills, but at least it's still something. I circle a few names of nannies and decide to call to interview them once I get a job.

Sunday afternoon I'm washing dishes when I hear a knock at the door. It can only be one of the Brownings, and I'm not in the mood to talk to them yet. The scene at Thanksgiving left me feeling raw. I wipe my hands on the dishtowel and open the door.

Valerie stands on my doorstep looking a little uncomfortable. She's a woman I worked with at the bar. I never gave her my address, so I'm surprised she's here. I'm also wondering why. I'm sure the shock shows on my face, because she fidgets before she speaks.

"Hey, Jill. I'm sure you're wondering why I'm here. It took me two days, but I finally got Dave the day manager to give me your address. I hated that I didn't say goodbye, and I didn't want that to be the end of our friendship. It's been a while since I've had a friend and well…"

I finally snap out of the shock and step to the side. "Come in."

"I don't want to bother you."

"You aren't. I'm glad you stopped by. I could use a friend, and I appreciate you going to all the trouble to find me."

"What the heck happened on Wednesday night?"

"Some guy got grabby and wouldn't take no for an answer. The bouncers weren't anywhere to be found, and my friend Johnny beat the guy up. When the bouncers couldn't give Johnny a guarantee that it wouldn't happen again, he flipped out and told me I had to leave. At first I was pissed, but then I thought about it, and he was right. I can't put myself in danger for a waitress job. I have to think about Mariah."

"Johnny got thrown out fighting for you? What is he to you?"

"Yes, he did. Long story. Short version is that he's Mariah's uncle. He helped me with a flat tire issue early in the evening, so he was there when I had problems with that guy. It was ugly. I've started looking for another job. We'll see how it goes."

"Well I know you don't have a lot of extra time, but do you think we could hang out sometime?"

I smile the first genuine smile in days. "Yeah, I think that would be great. I'll write my number down, and you can give me yours. I have a crappy old flip phone, so I don't text."

"Okay. Well, I should get going. I have to work in an hour. I'm glad you're okay. I was worried."

"We can try to get together this week if you have a night off."

"Just call me."

She slips out the front door and I smile, happy to have someone that I can call friend.

****

On Monday morning, I arrange with my boss to leave early until I can find someone to pick up Mariah. When I get to the daycare at five fifty-five, Judy is already there signing her out. My eyebrows squish together in confusion.

"What's going on, Judy?" I ask, wondering what in the heck she's doing here.

"I promised you when you moved here that I'd help you, so did John. We love having Mariah with us. It's our favorite part of the day. Please don't take that from us. We love her." Her bottom lip trembles, and she looks like she's about ready to lose it. She holds Mariah close to her and kisses her forehead.

"I tried to call you later on Thanksgiving Day and again the next two days. I'm sorry we upset you. I'm sorry I didn't stick up for you. You're not a burden to us, and we aren't too old to watch Mariah. We just let

Tara do it because we thought that's what she wanted. I'm sorry for that."

"It's not your fault. I hate that I've imposed on everyone, especially her. I knew she didn't like me. I just thought it was different for Mariah. I don't want to take her from you. You can see her whenever you want. I'm not going to take advantage of you anymore, though. That's gotten us nowhere good. I'm sorry I caused such a mess on Thanksgiving."

Judy, still fighting back tears, grabs my hand and pulls me outside. "Honey, you weren't taking advantage of us. I told you, and I'll keep telling you: We love having Mariah around, and we love helping you. You're a good mother, the best actually, you just need a little help, and we want to be the people to do that. I heard what Tara said and am embarrassed by her outburst, but it doesn't have much to do with you. She's been dealing with some things that none of us knew about. Just give her time. She'll apologize."

"She doesn't owe me anything, but after everything she said, I'm not comfortable having Mariah around her. I hope you understand that. Part of the reason I took you all up on the help you offered is because I want my daughter to have the kind of family I never did. My parents would never have done what you have for me. There was never any love in our home, never anyone to lend a helping hand and forgive mistakes, and never anyone to dry tears or give hugs. I want better for my daughter. You don't have to worry about weekend night duty anymore. I quit my job the night before Thanksgiving and haven't found a replacement yet. When I do, I'll just hire an overnight sitter. It's not a big deal, but if you could still help with the six o'clock pick up, I'd appreciate that. I was able to get off early today, but I had no idea what I was going to do the rest of the week."

"Jill, you don't want some stranger in your home alone with your daughter. Please let John and I keep her those nights. Tara spoke out of turn. We're not too old to watch her overnight, even if she's up crying. If I thought we were, I would tell you. John has always been good about sharing the nighttime crying baby duty. I usually take the first hour or two and then he gets up and switches with me. It's the only way we survived it when we were young. Besides, she usually sleeps through the night. Please?" Her eyes plead with me and I crumble.

"Okay, I guess. God, I just feel like I'm doing the wrong thing by saying yes. It's only going to cause problems in your family, and I don't want that to be on us. I'll let you know when I get another job, and we can work it out then."

"Well, now that you're off, why don't you let John and I take you to dinner. It'll just be the four of us. It'll be fun. I haven't been out to eat in months."

"Okay, that's fine. Let me go back in and get her stuff, then I'll follow you home."

While I'm at dinner with John and Judy, they ask a ton of questions about my family. It's unusual for me to talk about my brother because it's so painful, but I want them to understand what I grew up with so I tell them.

"My parents are ultra-conservative Christians who use their beliefs to judge and belittle rather than love and help. I learned at an early age that if I wasn't perfect, I'd pay. They were quick with the belt-beatings and tongue-lashings and slow with the hugs and love.

So slow, in fact, they were non-existent.

"I lived in their home until I was twenty-three years old because they said that good Christian women did not live alone because it invited sin into their lives or something like that. I was so terrified of them that I let them control me for that long into adulthood. They made me think that I couldn't live alone, that I wasn't capable, that I'd go straight to Hell if I did. Mind control is a scary thing, and they had that in spades.

"I finally left when my seventeen-year-old brother, Isaiah, committed suicide in our home. He left a note stating that he couldn't live with their 'judgmental tyranny' any longer. Instead of falling apart like you'd expect after the loss of a child, they went about their lives like business as usual and didn't say a word about it. We buried him on a Tuesday, and I moved out the following Monday. My parents were so mad they didn't speak to me for months, and when they did, it was only to judge me and say awful things, so I stopped all contact with them. Not that they seemed to care. I hadn't seen them at all in almost a year when they showed up at the hospital after the accident."

By the end of my story, John has stopped eating and Judy is watching me, her forehead wrinkled with concern.

John speaks first, "So what Johnny told us about the visit you got in the hospital from them after your accident is true?"

"I don't know what he told you, but I did tell him what happened, so I'm sure it's pretty accurate. According to them, Mariah is the spawn of Satan. That says it all, I think."

"You told us that part. They couldn't be more

wrong."

John reaches across the table and places his hand over mine. "You have us now, Jill. You don't need them, and you don't need to be alone. I know it's not easy right now. The circumstances of having you in our lives are complicated, and it will take time to work through that, but it'll be okay. Just always remember you have us."

Chapter Four

Jill

On Tuesday morning, I get a call while I'm at work from Mr. Bennett, my lawyer. Apparently, Lisa has petitioned the executor of the trust to change the distribution from six hundred dollars a month to one thousand. After I sit down and take a deep breath, I ask, "Why? I didn't ask for more money. I thought her first offer was generous enough."

"I have no idea. Her lawyer contacted me this morning and wanted to make sure you wouldn't protest it. I told him that wouldn't be a problem. It doesn't matter why. Once she changes it, she can't change it again without your permission so just take it and say thank you."

For the next few minutes, I sit on an upside-down bucket in a dingy janitor's closet and cry my eyes out. She keeps proving how amazing she is, over and over again. I do wonder what prompted her to ask for the change, but I'm afraid if I ask, I won't like the answer.

The best thing about the change is it means I don't have to work on the weekend. I can spend the whole weekend with my little girl from now on. That's a huge weight off my shoulders. I feel like I've missed so much already working those weekends.

****

Johnny

It's been a week since I've seen Jill, and it's really bothering me. I've seen Mariah every day, because I make it a point to go to my parents' to see her before she gets picked up. It makes me happy the way her face lights up when she sees me. Those chubby cheeks squish up with her toothless smile, and her beautiful brown eyes sparkle with happiness. I usually get to feed her, if I get there on time. Goofy noises are a hit while I'm trying to feed her and get her giggling. That little baby laugh of hers is the best sound in the world. If any of my buddies find out how I act during my time with her, I'll have to surrender my man card.

Giving Jill some space to calm down was a necessity when I realized my attempts to contact her weren't working. I feel like I've waited long enough though, so I'm going over there tonight after I'm certain she's put the baby to bed. I don't plan to leave until she talks to me.

Around nine o'clock, I knock on her door praying she'll answer. I wait a few minutes before I knock a second time, a little more boldly, and she finally opens the door. She's wearing a floor-length robe, no makeup and her hair is twisted up in some kind of complicated knot on top of her head.

"Johnny. What are you doing here?" Her arms are crossed defensively over her chest, her hip kicked out to the side, and her beautiful face set in a scowl.

"I've come to make peace. You won't answer my calls, so I decided I'd have to just show up. Can I come in, please?"

She steps to the side and ushers me in. God, she's gorgeous. I'd give anything to be able to tell her that, but she made it clear she doesn't want that kind of relationship with me. So, I have to respect that.

"Have a seat. Can I get you something to drink?"

"No, I'm okay. Will you listen for a minute?"

"I let you in, didn't I?" The snotty tone isn't typical for her, and I hate the sound of it.

"Yeah, but I can tell you're still upset with me, and I want to make sure you hear what I have to say."

"I'm listening."

"I'm sorry about the other night. I shouldn't have made you quit your job. It's not my business. I shouldn't have tried to take over and boss you. I know you need the money; I just worry about your safety. Drunk guys are assholes and can be dangerous. I'd kill someone if they hurt you.

"Kissing you was a mistake, and I'm sorry. I wanted to so badly, but it wasn't right, and it made you uncomfortable. I care about you so much more than you know, but I won't cross that line again. Please don't keep ignoring my calls. I've missed you this last week. You're my friend, and I enjoy our time together. I've been sneaking over to Mom's after she gets Mariah from daycare and leaving before you get there so I could see her without upsetting you, but damn it, I miss you and want to see you, too. I don't want to have to sneak around to see the baby anymore either. Can you forgive me?"

"I wasn't trying to keep Mariah from you guys, but after what I heard in the kitchen that day, I didn't want it said that I was using anyone or putting anyone out. I wish I'd known how your sister felt before. As for the job, you were right. It wouldn't be fair to Mariah if something bad happened to me if I was working in an environment I knew wasn't safe. Thank goodness I don't have to find another weekend job, though. My lawyer called me two days ago and said Lisa is increasing the monthly amount from Matt's estate to one thousand dollars. I don't know what made her do that, but I'll be forever grateful."

"Wow! Perfect timing. I hadn't heard about that from anyone, so I have no idea why she did it either. That's pretty amazing."

"As for the kiss, I can't blame you for that. I wanted it as much as you did. I knew it was wrong and went for it. I've missed you, too, but I still feel like you and I together are a bad idea. I want to be friends, but if that doesn't work for you, then I understand. It won't affect your time with Mariah, if that's what you decide."

"If you want to be friends, you can't stay away from me. What are you doing this Saturday?" I ask, sounding a little too eager.

"I thought about taking Mariah to the zoo. They have the Festival of Lights in the evening, and I thought she'd like that. Want to come with us? I think it will be fun."

"Yeah, why the hell not? What time does it start?"

"Five o'clock."

"Okay."

"Well then, how about I pick you two up at four, and we'll stop and grab something to eat and then head down there."

"That sounds good."

"All right, I'll let you get to bed. I know wake-up time comes early for you. I'll see you then."

She accompanies me to the door, and I hug her before I leave. I can't help myself. I just want to touch her, need to touch her, even if it's only for a minute. I pull away and leave without looking back. Being *just* friends isn't going to be easy.

****

Saturday comes and I pick the girls up. I broke down and bought a car seat for my truck like Steve did so we didn't have to wrestle hers into my truck every single time. That surprises her, but I just blow it off like it's what I should have done a long time ago.

Colorful Christmas lights are strung on all of the buildings, bushes, and fencing around the zoo. The laughter from happy children can be heard all over the park, and the smell of hot chocolate and cinnamon roasted almonds fills the air. Overall, the ambiance is festive and fun. I haven't been here in years and forgot how much I love the zoo.

Mariah seems to like the monkeys the most. Their exhibit stinks like hell, but it's worth the smell to see her reaction. At first, she just watches them walking around and doing monkey things until the one closest to us starts making noises and flipping around in the tree. Then she laughs her little head off. It's hysterical. We spend forever in there while she sits, fascinated.

It's cold outside, and Mariah is still young, so we end the night kind of early.

When I take them home, I help to get them inside and then leave quickly. If I stay, I'll be tempted to push Jill for more than she wants to give. I can tell she's disappointed or maybe just lonely not having a television or anything. As I sit in my car in her parking lot, I decide maybe it's time to find some female companionship. It's been awhile for me, and maybe if I handle that I'll relax a little.

I drive over to a little bar in a neighboring town that usually has some decent clientele on Saturday night and go inside. The place is busy, so I work my way through the crowd and get a drink. After about twenty minutes, a smokin' hot blonde sidles up next to me where I'm standing against a wall near the dance floor. She's about five feet six inches, long legs, slender, but stacked and not shy at all; she's perfect. She flips her long straight hair over her shoulder and flashes me a megawatt smile when she introduces herself as Mindy.

I tell her my name, and we talk for the next hour or so. A couple of drinks later she's on me. Her hands are on my chest, her lips are on my neck, and she's making sexy little noises that would normally have me looking for the nearest bed. She's really hot, but even I'm not cruel enough to sleep with one woman knowing I want someone else. When I arrived here at the bar, I thought I could do it, but the more I talked to Mindy the more I realized I don't want to be that kind of man. I decide to go ahead and cut out of there before I make a mistake. I walk her to her car, and we exchange numbers. Eagerly she accepts a date with me tomorrow night. I figure I can pick her up after dinner with my family.

****

The next day, I'm already at Mom and Dad's when Jill and Mariah arrive, so I help them unload their stuff and spend a good ten minutes just playing with Mariah on the floor. She's rolling all over the place and keeps getting up on her knees, rocking back and forth, but not crawling yet. It's like she can't figure out how to drag her knees across the floor to get going. It's hilarious until she gets pissed. Then I have to distract her with tickles and raspberries on her little Buddha belly to keep her from crying in frustration.

When I pull my face out of her tummy rolls, I see Steve standing just inside the room watching me. He laughs as he asks, "You've got it bad for both of them, don't you?"

"Nah, it's not like that. I do like Jill, and I adore this little lady, but we're just friends."

"Yeah, okay. Whatever you say, big brother. Do you know where I can find Jill? I need to talk to her. I haven't seen her since Thanksgiving."

My eyebrows lower in confusion. "Why didn't you call her?"

"I did. She wouldn't return my phone calls. I tried to stop by after dinner that night, too, but she wouldn't answer for me. Mary told me to give her a little longer and try again, so that's what I'm doing."

"I think she's in the kitchen with Mom."

My brother strides off in that direction, and I continue playtime with Mariah.

****

Jill

I'm standing in the kitchen at the center island with Judy slicing cucumbers when Steve comes in. I didn't know he was coming for dinner, or I would have declined the offer. I decided I am not going to push myself, or my kid, on anyone. It was obvious from the start that he wasn't crazy about me, and after what happened at Thanksgiving, I don't want to deal with him or Tara. You can't make people like you. They either do or they don't, so I have no plans to bang my head against the proverbial wall.

After he places a kiss on his mother's cheek, he steps up next to me, hip against the counter I'm working at and asks, "Can I please talk to you in private?"

I stop what I'm doing but never lift my eyes to his. I don't want to ruin another dinner. I can feel the panic building; I don't do well with confrontation

"I promise it won't take long. If you're more comfortable with my mom in the room, then we can talk here. Please?"

I take a deep breath and say, "You don't have to say anything to me. I won't make this awkward for you. If I had known you were coming, I wouldn't have come. I don't want to cause any more drama than I already have."

"Come on, just give me a chance, Jill. Listen to what I have to say. If you don't like it, I'll make sure I'm scarce when you're with my parents, okay?"

I debate the merits of getting this over with for about thirty seconds before I say, "Okay, that's fair."

We step out into the hall, and he leads me to a bedroom that I know was his when he lived here. There are trophies on shelves along the wall while pictures cover a corkboard of him with an array of people. There are a few posters, remaining clues that a teenage boy used to live in this space, plus a full-sized bed, a dresser, and desk. He motions for me to sit in the chair, and he sits on the edge of the bed. Now I notice that he's nervous. His hands won't stay still, and he keeps adjusting his legs.

"I'm sorry for how I've behaved, Jill. Let me give you a short history to help explain some things. In middle school, Lisa and I became friends. We spent all our time together. She was my best friend, but I had a major crush on her that I never told her about. I was afraid it would kill our friendship, but I was head over heels for her and stayed that way all through school.

"Our sophomore year, Matt asked her out. He knew how I felt, but he had to be the big man and do it anyway. We had a huge fistfight and then didn't speak for several weeks. It was bad. Not only did I lose my chance with her, I also lost my best friend because they started doing everything together. Things were never the same with Matt and me, or Lisa and me after that. We were still friends, but not so close anymore. I spent a lot of time being pissed at Matt. It wasn't until I met Mary that I got over it.

"Anyways, I knew that Matt was screwing around on her. I'm not sure how I knew. He never told me, and I could never prove it, but something was off with him. He had the same cocky demeanor that he had when he started seeing Lisa. I confronted him several times, and he lied to me every time. I knew he was lying to me, and I was so pissed at him we didn't even speak for the last three months he was alive because of it.

"When he died, I was angry at myself for being pissed at him and wasting the last year being ticked off with him for something I could never prove. That was until Lisa showed up here and told us about you. I was so angry with Matt and myself. I was pissed that Lisa was blindsided and hurt. I was furious that my brother was a liar and that I doubted myself. That's a lot of anger to build up. I've been sitting on all of that ever since.

"When my dad called for us to come help you, I was torn between wanting to make my dad happy and wanting to run from you. I was still angry, not necessarily at you, but at the whole situation. I'm obviously still very protective of Lisa, and I thought my loyalty should lie with her.

"When I showed up at your apartment in Indy, you were nothing like I thought you'd be. You were sweet, polite, thankful, and humble. You're also a rock. Probably the strongest woman I know, if all of the stories I've heard about you are true. I also noticed that you're an excellent mother. Your first priority has been Mariah since day one, and I think that's amazing. I couldn't ask for a better mother for my niece.

"Liking you was not on my agenda. I know it sounds childish, you can thank my wife for pointing that out. I just really felt that if I made friends with you, I'd be disloyal to Lisa, and I felt like one of the Brownings had to stay loyal to her. Yes, I realize that sounds asinine, and it was. I get that. When Lisa came to visit the day before Thanksgiving and as I was telling her about you and Mariah, I realized that I do like and respect you. I didn't get a chance to fix things before you left that day, because I walked into that whole scene a little too late. I don't feel the way my sister does. I don't even think she really feels that way, but she has to come to terms with whatever is in her head—I can't help her there.

"It was Lisa who encouraged me to get my head out of my ass and be a better friend to you. I should have been able to do that, but some things sit deep and take time to dig out.

"I love Mariah. That little girl is such a bright light in our family. It's the best thing my brother ever did, but I want you to know I care about you, too. It upset me that you were hurting on Thanksgiving.

"I don't know how to straighten up the shitty mess

I've made with you. I just want you to know that I'm sorry if I made you feel uncomfortable or less than welcome. It was uncalled for. Mary and I love having Mariah stay with us, so please don't stop that. It's not a burden for us at all, I promise."

My eyes filled with tears while he was talking. I understood things a lot better now, and to be honest, if I was Lisa's friend, I'd be super-protective of her, too. If it wasn't for her, I wouldn't have these people in my life.

"I didn't answer the door Thanksgiving because I was out walking with Mariah. I still don't have a television and didn't have any books, so I was bored. If I were home, I'm sure I would have answered. I was hurt and angry, but not enough to ignore a visitor.

"I understand why you were the way you were. I just hope you understand that I've been through so much. Between my own family and Matt, having a baby without a support system and no friends I could even call to talk to, every little thing after that just feels like more dirt on my grave. Mariah can still visit you guys. She loves being with you two, but I don't need to work nights anymore, so she really won't need to stay over."

"What happened with the job?"

"I quit after getting hit the night before Thanksgiving. That's a long story. One Johnny can fill you in on. I don't have to find another waitressing job because Lisa had the estate payments changed. I found out this past Tuesday. She upped it to one thousand dollars a month. I never heard why, but now I don't have to work weekends. I still have to work the job down in the city, which I don't mind, but I can spend time with my daughter on the weekends. Once my benefits start through work, I'll be able to put any extra into savings. I've hated not having that. Someday I'll find a way to thank Lisa."

"I think I know why she did that. When she was here, she asked how things were going. She was concerned that we wouldn't get much time with Mariah, so Mom told her you moved closer, and we were helping you with her while you worked an obscene amount of hours. When she asked why, we told her. I'm certain she changed it because she felt bad that there was a way to make things easier on you and give you more time with the baby."

"Matt was an idiot. Why would he cheat on her? I'll never understand why he came looking for me, wouldn't take no for an answer, and then kept coming back for a year when he had her. She's everything I've always wanted to be. I hate him for what he's done to everyone."

"Me, too. One minute I hate him for hurting everyone, and the next I feel guilty because he's my brother. It's messed up, no matter how you look at it. Can you forgive me for how things have played out with us?"

"Of course. I just didn't want you to feel you had to deal with me and take care of Mariah. I never want to be a burden for anyone. I spent too many years being one for my parents. I'm sorry I brought all of this to your family."

"You didn't bring anything to our family, but a sweet, happy baby and a kind heart."

He hugs me and leads me back to the kitchen. When his mom sees that I'm smiling this time, she kisses Steve on one cheek and pats the other one in a very motherly gesture.

"You're a good boy, Stevie."

"Thanks, Mom. I'm going to find the baby. Maybe I can steal her from Johnny."

The rest of the night went well. Tara and Bobby didn't show up, and I am so thankful for that. I know she still hates me. I'm sure that's bone deep and not something that will ever go away. Eventually, I'll face her again; I'm just not up to dealing with it yet.

Chapter Five

Jill
Two weeks later

Life has been getting better. I'm not as tired during the week since I have recuperation time on the weekend, and I'm happier being able to spend some time with Mariah. I hated never seeing her. Today I've decided to take Mary up on her offer to go Christmas shopping together. Steve is on baby duty, so I have a few guilt free hours to do this.

I'm stopped in the middle of the mall waiting for Mary to come out of a store when I spot Johnny walking out of Victoria's Secret of all places. I open my mouth to call out to him when a gorgeous, and I mean stunning, blonde saunters out of the store a few steps behind him. When he turns to face her, she dangles the bag in front of his face like candy. He smiles at her in a way that tells me he'll get to see what she just bought as soon as they get out of the mall. My heart plummets. It takes an all-out nosedive, and my stomach rolls like the tires on a Winnebago headed down the highway.

I shouldn't feel it, but I do. It's acid-burning, gut-churning jealousy. I'm standing there thinking that I can't feel any worse than I do right now until she tilts her head toward him, and he kisses her full on the mouth right in the middle of the mall. My heart cracks straight down the middle, and I know I have to get out of here before he sees me. I don't think I can keep a straight face if we run into them, so I turn and scan the crowd for Mary while moving back toward the store I came from. I'm praying that she's ready to go.

It's not my day, because the next thing I know Johnny's calling my name. I try to ignore it and pretend I can't hear him. Tears are threatening to flow, and I know my face is red. I walk a little faster until I'm snagged by the arm and jerked to a stop.

"Jill!" His gruff voice practically yells.

Shit. My shoulders sag in defeat. I paste on a fake smile and turn to face him.

"Johnny. Hey. What are you doing here?"

Oh God, did I really just ask why he's at a shopping mall? Of course, Miss Blondie-Perfect-Tits comes bounding up beside him, and I want to puke.

"Hey! I'm Mindy, Johnny's girlfriend," she says, all freakin' happy as she sticks her hand out to me.

I can feel my eyes widen as my brain tries to register what she just said. Wait…Wh…What? Did she say girlfriend? Oh my God, she did. Damn, I have to school my features quickly. I force a smile and shake her hand.

"Hi, I'm Johnny's niece's mom, Jill."

She's still bouncy happy as she starts yapping away about something, but I can't seem to focus on what the hell she's saying. All I can think about is the fact that she said *girlfriend*. It wasn't that long ago that he kissed me and told me he wanted to be with me. Now he has a girlfriend that looks like an overgrown Barbie doll?

Shit. Shit. Shit.

Thank God Mary shows up right about that time

and gets introduced to the girlfriend. When I glance at Johnny, hoping this encounter will end pronto, I notice he's studying me with a strange expression on his face. Then I realize Mindy's saying something else to me, so I try to tune back in.

"I'm sorry, Mindy, I missed what you just said," I say with as nice a tone as I can muster.

Miss Blondie-Perfect-Tits bounces a little on her toes and says, "Oh man, I'm so glad I met you guys today. I was stressing about dinner with the *fam* tomorrow. Meeting the family is a big deal. I feel better already."

I almost choke on my own saliva. She's coming to dinner at the Brownings' tomorrow? Oh, shit.

I'll never make it through an entire dinner with her there. I force a smile again and say, "Everyone there is really great. You'll be fine; don't worry. Well, Mary and I have to go. I promised Steve I'd be back to get the baby soon. Bye, Johnny. Bye, Mindy." I call the last over my shoulder as I drag Mary away, waving as we go.

We get around the corner, and she snatches me aside, away from the walking traffic.

"What the hell was that, Jill? Who was she?" Her tone is sharp.

I can tell she's half-irritated and half-confused.

I'm afraid I'm going to cry, so I swallow hard, hoping to hold it down.

"That was Johnny's new girlfriend. I just needed to go. We can see them tomorrow."

I already know I'll be cancelling that visit; I may have to pretend to be sick so I can avoid it.

"No, it's something else. What is going on? Come

on, you can talk to me," Mary pleads.

"Let's get out of here. I need a beer. I'll talk then."

Her eyes search my face. With a resigned sigh, she nods and replies, "Okay, a beer it is."

Fifteen minutes later, we're sitting at a quiet little bar, and she asks again, "What's going on?"

"I think I'm in love with Johnny. I didn't know he was dating anyone, and it took me by surprise. I don't think I was very successful at hiding my feelings."

"Why aren't you with him if you love him?"

She asks the question like the answer is so simple.

"Are you kidding?" I cough out a dry laugh. "Like my story with this family isn't fucked up enough. If we ever got married, my husband would be my baby-daddy's brother. That's an episode of Springer waiting to happen. What will people think? Why did I have to fall in love with him?" I whine and drop my forehead to my crossed arms on the table.

"First of all, I know he feels the same way about you. That's all that should matter. Not what it sounds like or what anyone will think. If you love him and he loves you, there shouldn't be a question about any of it."

"He doesn't love me, though, and now I never have a shot because he's got Miss Blondie-Perfect-Tits back there, and I have to sit at a dinner table with them tomorrow. It was going to be bad enough with Tara, who incidentally still hates me, but I don't want to face this, too." I groan and take a swig of my beer.

"After you left Thanksgiving Day, there was a big family throw down. Steve and I got there right on time for it. Apparently, Tara's issues with you have more to do with her own husband and her fear of his cheating or some shit."

"Who told you that?"

"John called her out on it. He lit her up one side and down another for treating you like crap. Right after that he told Steve off, who told him he'd already figured out he was being an ass for no reason. Then John told them all that Matt was dead, and he was a selfish prick. Just when we all thought he was done, he called Johnny out on falling in love with you. Said something like, '*If you really care about Jill and you think you can love her like she deserves, then go for it.*' He said they'd support you two, and that if he went for it, that he'd better plan on forever because you weren't the kind of girl for a one-night stand."

Slouching back in my seat, I groan again and look at the ceiling.

"We kissed the night I got fired. Okay, so kissing may be a light description of what we did. He's the best damn kisser I've ever laid my lips on, but I was afraid that being with him would make things worse with the family. I already felt like *persona non grata*, I didn't want to make it worse, so I told him we couldn't be anything but friends. He was pissed and left mad. Then everything went down the next day with Tara, and when he came to see me, he told me he knew we could only be friends, and he was okay with that. What his dad said must have hit home, because he backed right off."

"Oh, Jill. I'm sorry. I probably shouldn't have told you what John said, but it'll be okay tomorrow. You can sit by me, and we'll find something to distract you from her. I swear it will be okay."

"I'm such an idiot. I kept the Browning man that I

should have let go and let go of the one I should have kept. If he was really interested, he wouldn't have moved on already. How long has he been dating her? He just kissed me three weeks ago. Now he's bringing someone to meet the family? Oh God. I don't want to watch that. I don't think I can."

It takes Mary two shots, several beers, and over an hour for her to calm me down. By the time we get back to her house, there is no way I can drive and no way I should be left to care for an infant alone, so Steve makes me stay the night, and they promise to keep an ear open for Mariah. Mary gets me another beer when we get home, and I end up passing out in their guest room thirty minutes after they get the baby to bed in the portable crib.

I wake up the next morning feeling like I'm going to die, which helps keep me from lying when I decline to go to John and Judy's. I decide to keep Mariah with me since I didn't see her the day before. I've never been more relieved to be hung over in my life.

Around seven o'clock, I get a call from Johnny.

"Hello?"

"Hey, Jilli, you feeling okay?" His voice is heavy with concern.

I clear my throat and answer, "Yeah, I'm better. Should be back to new by tomorrow."

"We missed you today." He sounds sincere, but in the back of my mind, I'm thinking he wasn't missing me so much with Mindy there.

"Yeah, I missed seeing you guys today, too." Sadness tinges my voice, but I don't realize it until it's too late.

"What's going on? You sound weird."

"Oh, nothing. Just not all the way better I guess." I try to sound a little perkier this time.

"Are you sure? Because you were acting weird at the mall yesterday, too." He's not convinced.

"Oh, I must have just started feeling bad. I'm okay." After a long pause I blurt, "Mindy seems nice." I cringe realizing I may have given my issues away with that last sentence. Too late now. Damn.

It's silent on the other end of the line.

"Johnny?"

He answers more quietly, "Yeah I'm here. Mindy is nice. I missed seeing you and Mariah today."

"Yeah, we missed you, too. Listen, I'd better get going. I need to bathe Mariah and get her to bed."

"Okay, honey." My heart cracks at the sentiment. "You'd tell me if something was wrong, wouldn't you?"

"Yeah. I was feeling crappy, but I'll be okay. I always am. See you soon."

"Bye, honey."

"Bye."

I hang up the phone and fight off tears until I finally get the baby to bed. Then I cry until I fall asleep on my tear-soaked pillow.

As the next week and a half passes, I manage to avoid any dinner Johnny is at, but tomorrow is Christmas and I have to see him, and of course, since Mindy is now surgically attached to him, her also. I've decided that I won't ruin another holiday, so I'm going to paint on a smile and be nice as pie to Mindy and everyone else. Even Tara, who I haven't seen since Thanksgiving, will get my best pasted-on smile. It feels like the Christmas from Hell, and it hasn't even officially started. I figure I'll arrive a little bit late and leave a little bit early, then it won't be so bad. I just keep reminding myself that I'm doing this for Mariah. I'm giving her the loving family I never had.

Christmas turns out to be a nice day even if it's a bit awkward. Mindy sits on Johnny's lap every chance she gets and hand feeds him little snacks when his mouth is within reaching distance. It makes my chest ache, but I try to laugh when everyone else does and hide the feeling of black sludge resting in my gut. Mary does her best to distract me and pull me from the room often, for little tasks that she supposedly needs help with.

As soon as I can, I excuse us for the night, saying I need to get to bed since I have to work the next day. I wasn't supposed to work. Because it's the day after Christmas and my boss offered me time and half to let the electricians in to fix some wiring in a couple of the classrooms, I accepted. Doing so also gave me the added bonus of opting out of the post-holiday affair at the Brownings'. They're all off work and, from what I've been told, spend the day together every year. I knew I wouldn't be able to handle two days in a row of the sappy, lovey moments of Johnny and Mindy.

The next day I drop Mariah off with Judy around eight o'clock and drive to work. The electricians are waiting for me when I arrive, so I let them in and show them where everything is. The supervisor's name is Chris, and he is really good looking. His hair is a dirty blond and on the longish side. He's probably a little older than I am with a nice smile and kind eyes. He's about six feet tall and maybe a hundred and ninety pounds. He's muscled without being ripped, and he flirts with me like crazy. That boosts my spirits a little; every girl likes a little flirting now and then.

Right before he leaves for the day, he asks for my phone number. I debate giving it to him but decide I have nothing to lose at this point. Mindy looks like she's here to stay, and sitting around waiting for her to go away is wasting my time, not to mention there is still the issue of me being Johnny's dead brother's ex-girlfriend.

I give Chris my number, and he says he'll call.

****

Johnny

Something's going on with Jill, and I have no idea what it is. It started a few weeks ago, and everyone keeps telling me she's fine, but I know she's not. I just don't know why. I figured I'd talk to her at Mom's, but she hasn't been around as much, and yesterday we were never alone long enough to talk. Granted, Tara was in the room yesterday, and I don't think that's happened since she went off on Jill at the last holiday gathering, but it's something else.

Mindy and I have been seeing quite a bit of each other, but I think we need to cool it, and I plan to tell her that tonight. She's a nice woman, a lot of fun, always happy, but wants to spend every waking moment with me. I'm feeling smothered, and I don't like it. I've been a bachelor a long time and am used to having some space. There is something to be said for basic breathing room. She's showed up at work several times unannounced. At first I thought it was sweet, but since then, I've gotten the feeling it's more to see what I'm doing and who's there. Last week I was in the shop explaining to a client the repairs I made to her car when

Mindy showed up. Granted, the client is young and beautiful, but the conversation was purely business so when Mindy waltzed over and interrupted by sticking her tongue down my throat and hanging on me, I decided I'd had enough. She probably should have just pissed on me like a dog, marking her territory. It would have been less embarrassing. I pride myself on professionalism, so that did not go over well with me. After the client left, I explained my feelings about her actions, and she blew me off.

She's been pushing to make things more serious between us, and I'm just not interested. Part of it probably has to do with the fact that she's not Jill and the other being that she doesn't really fit in with my family. She invited herself to meet them a few weeks ago and somehow did the same for Christmas. Everyone was nice to her, but something about her just doesn't mesh with my family, and it leaves me feeling awkward and quiet when we're all together.

She's gotten really pushy about sex all of the sudden. I realize we're adults, and it's probably weird that I've been seeing her this long and haven't sealed the deal, but every time we start to get hot and heavy, my brain drifts to Jill, and I throw the brakes on. The whole situation is jacked up so I feel like it's time to end things with her. That conversation is going to suck.

When I'm done talking to Mindy, I plan to corner Jill and find out what the hell is going on. Something she said or maybe it was the way she said it during our phone call a few weeks ago made me wonder if she was upset about Mindy. I couldn't figure out what about Mindy would have upset her since their interactions so far seem to be friendly. If it were anyone else, I'd think she was jealous, but I know Jill doesn't want to date me. She made that very clear.

****

Jill

I pick up Mariah from Judy and head home. As I'm struggling to carry her in the car seat and her diaper bag into the apartment, my cell phone rings. I fumble around a bit and finally get it out of my purse. I don't recognize the number, but answer anyway.

"Hello?"

A deep sexy voice responds, "Hello, Jill. It's Chris from earlier at the school."

"Oh, hi Chris. Give me just a second so I can get in the door."

"Okay."

I release a tired breath and say, "Okay, let me put my daughter down, and I'll be right with you."

I put the car seat down, shut, and lock the door before I sit down on the floor in front of Mariah. She's smiling at me like she's never been happier.

"Okay, I'm back."

"You have a daughter?" He sounds a little shocked.

"Yes, she's seven months old."

"Are you married?"

Seriously? Did he really just ask that? That's kind of offensive.

"Um, no. I wouldn't have given you my number if I were." I'm sure he can tell I'm not happy about his question.

"I'm sorry, that was a stupid question. I just thought with how young the baby is I might have missed something."

"No. Her dad died before she was born. I'm single.

I've been that way since I was only a couple of months pregnant." I don't want to have a discussion about this with him.

"Oh, okay. I'm not trying to pry. I just wanted to make sure there wasn't going to be a husband or boyfriend hunting me down for calling," he says with a nervous laugh.

"Nope, you're safe."

"Well, I was wondering if I could take you to dinner tomorrow night. I know that's really soon, and it may be hard to find a sitter, but I had to ask. I didn't want to wait to see you again."

In my mind, I'm thinking that I don't want anyone but Johnny, and then I remind myself, sadly, he has Mindy.

"Sure, that sounds nice."

"Okay. I'll take you to a nice restaurant down on the river for dinner. Is seven okay?"

"Yes, I'll be ready."

We finish up the call by me giving him my address and saying we'd see each other tomorrow night. I hang up the phone and call Mary. First, I ask if they can babysit. They can, so that helps. Then I tell her about my date. She tells me she'll be over around two o'clock with a few dresses to choose from and to help me get ready. I think she's just excited I have something to do besides mope around about Johnny and Mindy.

Chris shows up the next night a little bit before seven o'clock, and he's dressed like an Abercrombie ad. He looks nothing like the blue-collar worker I met yesterday. He is handsome, though.

"Jill, wow, you look amazing!"

"Thank you. You clean up nicely yourself."

With a flash of a grin and a hand at the small of my back, he leads me to his car and opens the door for me. Dinner is excellent, and I find that Chris is very funny.

Johnny calls twice through dinner, and I ignore both. Shortly after the second one, I excuse myself to the ladies' room to listen to the voicemails. There isn't anything urgent, so I decide to call him back tomorrow. If my phone was newer I'd text him, but it's still this stupid flip phone, and it seems to take an hour to send a short message so I decide he can wait.

At the end of the evening, Chris walks me to my door, and I get those goofy little butterflies flapping and swarming uncomfortably in my stomach. They're the kind that show up right before a first kiss. I'm really nervous. Thank goodness Chris makes it easy; he doesn't make small talk or hesitate. He just goes for it. His lips are soft, but commanding. It's a nice first kiss. Not too much, not too little.

The only problem is that it's not Johnny's mouth on mine which leaves me feeling a little sad instead of excited. When he leaves, he asks if he can see me again, and I just tell him to call me. He says he will and then ambles back to his car. I don't know if it's a good idea to go out with him again knowing I'm in love with someone else.

Chapter Six

Jill

After I let myself inside, I twist the lock on the door and hear the *thunk, thunk, thunk* of a heavy-handed knock. I figure it's Chris, so I open it back up with a smile and instead find Johnny standing there with a scowl on his face.

My smile fades and I ask, "What are you doing here, Johnny?"

His eyes narrow on me.

"You wouldn't return my calls, so I came to see why. You wouldn't answer your door, so I called Steve to see if he'd heard from you, and he said you were out on a date, and they had Mariah."

"Okay, so you figured out why I didn't call you back, but that doesn't explain why you're here this late. Shouldn't you be with Mindy?"

Irritation flashes in his eyes and he says, "No, I'm here to find out why you've been avoiding me, and why you didn't return my calls tonight. What's going on? Do you think you can let me in so the whole complex doesn't hear this conversation?"

Stepping back, I usher him inside and close the door behind him.

"Nothing is going on. I listened to your messages, and they didn't sound urgent. I figured I'd call you tomorrow when I wasn't in the middle of a date. If I had a better phone, I would've texted you to let you know, but I still have that piece of shit phone for a few more months and texting is a nightmare. Now, what's so important that made you go to all this trouble?"

"I want to know what's wrong with you. You've been avoiding me for weeks, and I don't know why. I'm tired of it. I miss seeing you. Now, what's going on?"

"Nothing is going on. I've been busy. That's all."

My eyes shift to the ground. I can't look him in the eyes while I flat-out lie.

"Busy doing what? Out with lover boy?" He sneers, and I notice his clenched fists hanging at his sides, his tense shoulders, and the irritability rolling off him in waves.

"That was my first date with Chris. I've just been busy. Why does it matter? You still get to see Mariah even when I'm not around."

"Yeah, Mariah is around. I've seen her plenty, and I love it, but I haven't seen *you* and I miss you. Did I piss you off?"

I raise my eyebrows, a little surprised at his words and his accompanying grumpy tone.

"No. Everything is fine. I'll make more of an effort. I promise."

"I must have done something. Everyone else except Tara sees you all the time. Tell me what the fuck is going on!" His voice started a little loud, but he finishes on a yell startling me. This is very unlike him. "Come on, Jill. What's the deal?"

His chest is heaving with irritated exertion, and his cheeks are pink. His anger, his raised voice, and his attitude piss me off, so I finally snap. He's badgered me into a corner, and I'm done. My brain shuts down, and my instant reactions report for active duty.

That's never a good thing.

"I can't watch you with Mindy! I can't fucking do it!" I yell back at him. "I did my best. I just can't fucking stand it. I don't want to make her feel bad or be rude, but I don't have a clue what's going to come out of my mouth when she's in the room."

I know my face is red. It always gets that way when I get mad. I'm breathing heavy, and I'm watching as his expression morphs from pissed to questioning. He steps closer to me. Close enough that I can smell his cologne, laced with a hint of mechanic probably left over from work today, and it makes my knees weak, but I try not to physically react. I'm mad at him for pushing me to tell him this stuff.

"What are you talking about?" His voice is low and a little intimidating.

He bends his neck trying to make eye contact with me as I steadily look at anything but him.

"I just told you. I don't want to talk about this anymore. Can you go now?" I plead with him.

"No. Fucking. Way. You've been avoiding me because you don't like Mindy? She's sweet, and she's nice to you, so I don't see the issue. How fucking stuck-up are you?"

"Are you kidding me? I'm not stuck up. I'm in love with you, jackass. I can't watch her kiss your goddamn face one more time. I can't listen to her pet names for you, and I can't watch her feed you one more piece of food from her fingers. I want to break those damn things off every single time!" I close my eyes and lower my chin to my chest realizing I laid it all out there.

Shit.

"What did you just say?"

He steps in even closer to me. His hands go to my shoulders holding me in place.

Silence ensues as I continue to look at my feet unable to meet his eyes.

"Seriously, what did you say?" he asks louder this time.

"I'm jealous, okay. I can't watch you with her. Yes, she's nice. Yes, she's a freaking bombshell, but I can't do it," I end on a whisper.

I'm ashamed of my thoughts and actions.

"Jealous? You say you love me, but a month ago, you told me you just wanted to be friends. I'm confused here, Jill. You don't want me, but you don't want anyone else to have me either?" His voice goes up an octave. "That's pretty damn selfish, don't you think?" He shakes his head in disgust. "And I want to know why, if you're so in love with me, you went out with that douchebag tonight?"

"He's not a douchebag. He's a nice guy. He asked me out, and I thought if I went out with him, I wouldn't be so jealous over you."

His eyes flame with irritation.

"Did it work? Did whoring with someone else do the trick?"

I can feel the color drain from my face as my stomach rolls over at his words.

"Whoring? Are you kidding me? The guy kissed me once. We weren't shopping at Victoria's Secret for slut-wear for me to show him tonight."

Direct hit. And he knows it. That's what he and Mindy were doing at the mall that day.

His attitude spikes again as he asks, "So what? Now I'm just supposed to dump her because you finally admit you love me?"

"No," I whisper. "I didn't want to tell you. I know you've moved on. I just wanted to avoid you until I stopped feeling this way."

A single tear slides down my cheek, and I see a crack in his hard-ass-drunk-guy routine for about a second then it pops back into place. "Is that your thing, Jill? Do you like to play games and jerk guys around? Is that how things played out with Matt? Is that why he left? He thought the baby was another game?"

That's the killing blow right there. I'm done. I sink down and drop to my behind on the linoleum floor of the kitchen, wishing the world would end right now. I'm never going to get past what happened with Matt. I'm always going to be the girl no one loves or even likes for that matter; the dumbass who got knocked up by a married man.

"You can go." I choke out as I wrap my arms around my knees and pull them close to my chest.

He stands still, but I won't look up to meet his eyes. The words he uttered, I can't come back from. It's all of my worst fears said aloud from the one person I didn't want to feel that way. My whole life I've been told I'm a useless piece of shit. Just ask my parents. Or my friends. Oh, wait; I don't have any of those. Ask Matt or Lisa or Tara. Now you can even ask Johnny. I curl up in a ball on the floor, but I don't cry. I've gone numb.

****

Johnny

Fuck. Fuck. Fuck. I was pissed and went too far,

and now I don't think I can fix it. I watched her shut down right in front of me, and now she's curled into a little ball on the floor. I don't know what to do. I'm so pissed I want to throw stuff or punch holes in the walls, but I don't want her to look like that. I can't believe I said that. I'm not sure where that even came from.

I walk over to her with timid steps and bend down. "Jill. Jillian?"

She doesn't answer. Her eyes are fixed straight ahead, and she's not seeing anything. It's like she just vacated her body.

"Jillian? Come on, honey. I'm sorry. I never should have said that. It's not true. I was just mad. Please, look at me. Jill?"

Nothing.

Shit, shit, shit.

"Please, Jillian. I'm sorry. I swear I didn't mean it."

"Just leave, please." Her raspy voice is heavy with unchecked emotion.

"I'm not going anywhere. We have to talk this out. I said I'm sorry. Please sit up and talk to me."

"I've got nothing left, Johnny. Go home."

Her body is limp on the floor. She's not crying, and I think that may be worse than if she were. Her voice has an odd tone when she speaks, and I pray I never have to hear that sound again.

I stand up and pace back and forth for a few minutes. She never moves. If she hadn't spoken that little bit to me, I'd think she went catatonic. It's the spookiest shit I've ever seen.

I can't leave her like this. I'm terrified of what she'll do. I try again.

"Jill, come on, honey. Sit up and talk to me. Yell at me. Something. Don't shut me out. The shut out is what started this in the first place."

I'm pleading now, and I hate the way it sounds, but I'll do anything to wipe that look off her face.

After several more minutes of continued silence, I slide an arm under her back, the other one under her legs and carry her to her room. She doesn't say a word or move at all. I take her boots off and see that she's wearing pantyhose, so I lift her dress enough to assess that she's wearing the thigh high kind, and I carefully roll them down her beautiful legs to remove them. Still no response so I cover her up, kick my shoes off, and crawl in behind her to spoon up close. I'm probably taking my life in my own hands, but at this point at least a freak-out would be some kind of reaction.

God, I've fucked up so bad this time. I acted like my asshole brother and treated her like every other person in her life. I wanted to be different. I wanted to treat her with the love and respect she deserves, but instead I yelled at her and said a bunch of things I can't take back. Things I knew would hurt her.

I lie here running my fingers through her hair telling her how sorry I am. I know without a doubt I've broken this poor girl with my careless words. I forget how fragile she is sometimes because she's overcome so many obstacles in her life, ones that would likely kill the rest of us. She just keeps getting up and fighting her way through the tough stuff, but something about tonight has me thinking she doesn't want to fight anymore and knowing what happened with her brother I'm afraid to leave.

I spend most of the night awake, running fingers

through her hair, over her arms, and face, too. I'm trying to be soothing, but I can't tell if it's working. My big ol' calloused hands aren't meant to touch skin this soft, but it's the only thing I can think to do. I'm so damn sorry, and I keep saying it, but it's obvious that she's not okay. I wish she'd yell at me, or something.

Sometime close to dawn, Jill rolls to her back, eyes seeking mine. She never says a word just strokes my jaw with her fingertips. Her eyes hold a sadness I've never seen before, and I know I shouldn't, but I can't seem to help myself, so I close the distance between us slowly. I'm waiting for her to push me away, but she doesn't. Our lips touch, and it's a soft brush, a small connection. As I pull back to observe her response, her eyes shift to my lips, and she lifts her head to kiss me again. There is more behind it this time—more passion, more expectation, and a lot less control.

Both of her hands grip my hair, and she tugs it. Her aggression is a major turn on, and I realize I may not be able to stop this even if I want to. Her knee slides up the side of my leg and hooks over my hip locking the hard-on I've developed in the last thirty seconds with her soft center. Instinctively, I rock into her, and a breathy moan escapes her lips.

I run my hand up under her skirt and palm the firm cheek, squeezing her ass as I roll my hips against her. Then I trace a soft path with my fingers over her skirt, under her blouse, encountering the incredibly soft skin of her ribs until I reach the bra she's still wearing from last night. The texture on my fingers says it's lace, and that knowledge stokes the fire that's burning inside me for her. I sweep my thumb across her covered nipple and smile as it hardens at my touch.

I sit up and guide her with me, helping to shuffle her out of the outfit from last night, which I toss to the floor. She's sitting in front of me in a maroon lace bra and matching bikini panties. I wrap my fingers in the shirt collar at the back of my neck and pull it over my head. Then I stand quickly and remove my jeans, leaving me in only my boxer briefs. Her eyes shift and take in my nearly naked form and widen briefly before she meets my eyes again.

"Johnny." Her voice is breathy and quiet.

I reach for her and trace a gentle finger over the swell of her perfect breasts. Her chest rises and falls as she watches the motion of my hand. I tease her nipple with light circles and shift to the other breast. I'm taking things at a snail's pace. I'm touching her the way I've wanted to for so long, praying the whole time she doesn't put a stop to this.

I shift so that I'm kneeling between her spread legs. She's on her elbows now, legs bent at the knees, watching me with hooded eyes. No words are exchanged. Coasting my hands up her silky legs, I hook my fingers in the sides of her sexy panties, tug them down her legs, and toss them toward her skirt. At the sight of her bare, glistening sex, my cock jumps. I lean in to inhale the scent of her sex and lick her outer lips with gentle strokes. Her body twitches while her eyes blaze.

Parting her tenderly, I stroke her inner folds with my tongue until she's grinding into me, silently begging me for more. When I think she can't take any more, I lock my lips around her clit and suck hard, watching her reaction from the perfect location. She cries out as she thrashes and writhes while I hold her thighs captive and wring her of all pleasure.

I crawl up her body as she relaxes like a wet noodle against her sheets. I slide my arms around to her back and remove her bra. I truss up her beautiful lush breast with my hand and swirl my tongue over the taut nipple, my eyes raised to her, watching for her reaction. I close my lips over it giving it a little nip. Her hips buck, but she never opens her eyes. I do it again, working for more of a reaction. I get the same result, so I graze her with my teeth, and her eyes pop open to meet mine, her libido coming back to life. *Got her!*

I'm gentle as I lick my way over to the other breast, do the same thing in sequence, and get the same reaction, with the added bonus of her legs parting farther this time. Her hips rise to make contact with me. I shuffle the boxers off and look at her waiting for permission. She's quiet at first, studying my face.

Her eyes never leaving mine she asks, "Are you still sleeping with Mindy?"

"I never was. Even with her around I still only wanted you."

"Why? She's hot, and she wants you."

"She's not you."

That answer must work for her because she locks her legs around my back and rolls her damp sex against me.

"I need you, Jill. Do you want me?"

She nods. Tears fill her eyes, and when I try to put a halt to it all, given her reaction, she shifts lining up her wet core with my rock hard cock. All warnings and reason go out the window, and I lose my mind momentarily. When I thrust into her, she cries out and arches up.

"Johnny!"

I have never felt anything better. She clenches me from within, and I suddenly realize I didn't wrap it. Every muscle I have locks up tight. *What the hell am I doing?* A few hours ago, we were yelling at each other, and then she stopped speaking to me altogether. Instant reality check, I just fucked up on so many different levels. I'm taking advantage of her compromised state of mind.

I pull out quickly, startling her, and jump off the bed. She looks confused and vulnerable as a stray tear rolls down her cheek.

"Johnny, don't leave me like this," she pleads.

"You don't want this. Not with me. It's been an emotional night. We aren't thinking straight. I don't want to take advantage of you. I don't want you to regret this later, and I know you will. A few hours ago, you wouldn't even look at me. It's not right."

"Johnny, come back to bed. You can leave me in the morning and go back to your life. Right now I need you; I need this."

I don't want to hurt her more, and I honestly don't want to miss this chance. My mind is at war with my body. I'm selfish as I make my decision and lean over digging into my wallet to produce a condom. I roll it on and settle back between her legs. More tears slip out of her eyes, and I swipe them away with my fingers. Concern niggles at the back of my mind, but her warm flesh is beneath me, her eyes pleading, and my body is screaming for release so I ignore it.

I rock back inside of her at a leisurely pace this time, and her legs lock behind my back again. Her fingers trail over the dusting of hair on my chest, up and over my neck, touching every inch of skin she can reach. My thrusts are slow, grinding our hips together as I bottom out inside of her. I'm building the pleasure between us, and her moans increase as my pace does. She squeezes me from inside and just as I'm about to explode, her eyes roll back, every muscle in her body tenses and she screams my name. That primal sound pushes me over the edge, and I thrust several more times, as I empty myself into the condom.

I bury my face in her neck and kiss the salty skin. Then I take her lips one long last time before I get up to remove the condom. When I come back to bed, she's on her side facing away from me. I move in behind her and spoon up with one arm sliding under her head and the other arm across her waist. I kiss her exposed shoulder blade, but she doesn't say another word. That should be my clue that something isn't right, but I'm cum-spent and drowsy.

An hour or so later, I feel her get out of bed. The door to the bathroom clicks shut, and I sit up on the side of the bed with the sheet pulled across my lap. I know we need to talk. There are a million things I need to say. I'm just not sure where to start and fatigue eats at my senses.

After she's done, she stands in the doorway and surprises me by saying, "I think you should go. Thanks for staying with me. I'm okay. I know you're sorry. I am too, but I need to be alone for a little while before I go pick up the baby."

I step away from the edge of the bed letting the sheet hit the floor and position myself in front of her. She must have tugged her robe on while she was in the bathroom, because she's covered from neck to toe now.

I'm still stark naked, but it doesn't matter since she won't look at me, not at my body and certainly not in my eyes. My chest seizes with internal panic.

"Please look at me."

She looks up at me, but her expression has a vacant sign posted.

"What happened with us in bed means something to me. Don't push me away now. I'm sorry for all the things I said during our fight. I didn't mean them. I was pissed. I was hurt, and I was jealous."

I finally get a reaction from her, but it's in the form of tears. They fill her eyes and spill down her cheeks without a sound.

"I know you didn't mean it. It's okay. I just really need some time before Mariah comes home. Okay? Don't worry about me. I'll be fine." Her voice is wicked quiet as she tells me this.

"I'm serious. What we did means something to me. I want to talk about this; I don't want to leave you upset. Please, don't make me go while you're like this."

"I'm fine. I'll be okay. I just need some time. It was a long night. Really, it's okay. It was one night. You have a girlfriend you have to go back to today. I'm sorry for that, by the way. I guess I'm just born to be the other woman." Her self-deprecation pisses me off.

"Don't say that. It's not true. I'm not with her any more. I called it off with her before I came here. I wouldn't do that to you or her. Please! It doesn't have to be one night." It feels like I'm begging her.

"You ended it with her?" She's skeptical.

"Yes. I told you. I knew I didn't love her. It's you I want."

"I need some space. I need to think about all of

this. Last night was too much for me. I know you apologized, but the things you said to me won't just go away. I never should have been with Matt, but I still question everything in that relationship from how it started to how his life ended. You say you didn't mean what you said, but the words came from somewhere within you. Although I'd like to be pissed at you for saying them, they may be the truth. I have too many things to come to terms with."

"I didn't mean it. I don't know how else to tell you that. Please believe me."

"Johnny." She steps forward, slides her arms around my waist, and places her head on my chest.

In a low voice she says, "I'm in love with you, but I hate myself. It makes me question everyone and everything around me. I need some time. Please give me that."

I relent. If she wants her space, I have to respect that, but I hate it. My chest tightens like it's in a vice as I throw my clothes on and walk out her door. Everything in me says I need to stay here and fix what I helped to break, but I can't force her to want that.

I head to Steve's house for some advice. I'm not sure what to do about any of it. When I arrive at Steve's, Mariah is in the highchair and he's feeding her breakfast. Mary must still be asleep because the rest of the house is quiet.

"What's up, man? Why you up so early? You look like shit."

"I fucked up. Big time."

"What do you mean?"

"I went by Jill's last night when she wouldn't return my calls. She's been avoiding me for weeks, and

I was fed up with it. I waited until she got back from her date. That guy was a douchebag, by the way. Once he left, I confronted her, and we had a fight. A nasty one. She told me she was in love with me and couldn't watch me with Mindy. Then I told her she liked to play games, and that's probably why Matt left. At one point, I accused her of whoring around with that guy last night."

My brother spins on his chair to face me. "What the fuck, dude? Are you kidding me? Why would you do that?"

"I don't know. I was pissed, jealous, and really mad, and it just came out. It was after the Matt comment that she just sort of shut down. She wouldn't talk. She just lay on the floor. It was scary; I've never seen anything like it."

"Of course she shut down. You just hit the jackpot on worst things that you could ever say to a girl like her. Damn, you're a fucking idiot. You know better than anyone in our family what her life has been like. Mary has spent some time with her and has given me some detail. Man, no one has ever been kind to her. She has no one but us. This is jacked up."

"That's not the end of the story. I ended up sleeping with her, too. I'm not sorry for that. It's her I want, and she knows it. I told her after the fact. She told me she loves me, but she hates herself, and it makes her question everything and everyone. She asked me for some time to think. I left her to it, but I didn't want to."

"Dude, you screwed this up pretty bad."

"I know, but I don't know how to fix it. I told her I was sorry a thousand times, but she woke up this morning and said it was okay and she was sorry, too.

Then she told me to leave. She said she needed time alone. I begged her to let me stay, but she wouldn't. I don't know what to do. She was eerily quiet and withdrawn."

"Yeah, well you dealt her a verbal blow last night, and that was probably the straw that broke the camel's back for her. Then you slept with her and confused her. I'll talk to Mary when she gets up and have her check on Jill. That's the best I can do. Give it a few days and try to talk to her again, but I suggest that you don't resort to name-calling anymore with her. It seems to be the one thing she can't handle. I'm assuming that goes back to her parents and whatever went on in that house."

****

Instead of going home, I go to my shop and work for most of the day. I clean up and drive to Mom's for dinner. When I get there, I find out Jill has cancelled for the day saying she wanted to spend the day with Mariah. Mary and Steve exchange concerned looks with me, but stay quiet.

As I'm contemplating Jill's absence, Bobby reaches over and grabs hold of Tara's hand. She clears her throat and says, "I'm pregnant. We're gonna have a baby!" We all give them hugs and congratulations. They've been trying and were getting frustrated with how slow the process was for them. Thank goodness Tara and Bobby seem to be doing better. There is a lot of smiling and touching that wasn't there for a long time. I'm glad to see my sister happy again. Now it would really help if she made up with Jill.

****

Two weeks go by and I don't see Jill at all. It's

killing me not to go over there, but Mary has reiterated the importance of giving her space. Mindy has tried calling me several times. I only returned the first one, and that was to make sure she knew I had no plans to get back together with her. I was nice about it, but I was firm. That conversation was difficult, so I'm avoiding having to do it all over again. Why she continued to call after the first conversation, I don't know.

I still see Mariah almost every day, because I go to Mom's to see her before she gets picked up. It's during the third week that I finally see Jill. My mom has a doctor's appointment in the afternoon and wants my dad to go with her after work, so I agree to pick up Mariah and watch her until they get back. Around seven o'clock, my mom calls to check on me, and when I tell her everything is okay, she says they'll leave her with me so they can have dinner out. About seven-forty, Jill comes through the door.

"Hey." She says it like she sees me all the time and gives a small smile I know is fake, because it never reaches her eyes.

I stand up holding Mariah who goes bonkers trying to get out of my arms to her mother. Jill gives her a genuine smile, and then her expression slides back into the same bland one she was wearing when she entered.

"Where's your mom?"

"She had a doctor's appointment, and then she and Dad went to dinner."

"I would have skipped the overtime if I'd have known you had to stay with her. I'm sorry."

My brows knit together. "Why would you do that? I don't mind keeping her. In fact, I love it. I come to see her almost every day she's here anyway. I just leave before you get here because I didn't think you wanted me around. I'll keep her anytime you need help."

She studies me for a few extra seconds and says, "Okay, well, I need to get her home. Thanks for watching her. Is Judy okay? She never mentioned an appointment to me."

"I don't know. She just called me earlier and asked me to watch her, and I agreed. I'll ask when she gets home."

"Take care, Johnny."

"Wait, Jill. Are you feeling okay? You don't seem to be yourself."

She gives me the fake smile thing again and says, "Yeah, I'm okay. Just some trouble sleeping, but I'll be fine. This happens sometimes. Thanks for asking."

She shuffles out the door before I can say or ask anything else. Something still isn't right. That's not the woman I know. She wasn't mad, sad, happy, silly, or stoic. She was vacant, like the day I left her apartment after our fight. Totally void of emotion and her appearance alarms me, too. She's lost some weight and has dark circles under her eyes. I'm worried about her, and I'm not sure how to approach her. She's been avoiding Sunday dinners with the family. I've heard that she's eaten with Mom and Dad a couple of times during the week since the last time I saw her, though. I'll give her a little longer to process whatever this is, and then I'll make her talk to me again. If nothing else, I'm learning patience with her.

Two days later, I'm in the middle of chowing on my sandwich during my lunch break when my phone rings.

"Hi, Mom."

"Hey, Johnny. Any chance you can pick up Mariah and watch her till Jill gets here tonight?"

"I wish I could, but I'm backed up. There are three cars due back to customers tomorrow, and Josh is out sick."

"Okay. I'll call Steve and Mary. Good luck, honey."

"Thanks, Mom. If you can't get anyone just call me back, and I'll break until she gets picked up."

"Don't worry, I'm sure Steve and Mary can help."

She ends the call quickly, and I finish my lunch.

****

Jill

I turn into the Brownings' driveway, and for the second time this week, Judy's car is gone, and one of the kids' cars is here. This time it's the other one I don't want to see. Tara. I'm praying she hasn't been here long. I don't want Mariah around people who don't love her, and she's still young enough I can make that happen. She'll get plenty of nastiness later on in life.

I push the door open and walk through the foyer to the family room where I find both Bobby and Tara on the floor with her. Mariah is army crawling across the floor, which is something new. It's almost like she got sick of trying to crawl the right way and improvised.

Tara is laying out in front of her with her phone on video mode recording her movements. Bobby is lying where I guess she started, laughing at her antics. I stand still at the end of the couch watching all of this with a weird fascination when Mariah changes direction at the sight of me and pulls herself all the way over to me. I pick her up and snuggle her chubby little cheek telling her how much I love her and how much I missed her.

127

Tara sits up and says, "I could tell she was about to do something cool so I got out the video camera so you wouldn't miss it."

My mouth drops open, and I stare at her like she sprouted five heads. The last time, other than Christmas, that I saw her was our big throw down. I'm not quite sure what to make of this. Finally, I snap out of it and say, "Thank you. I'd love to see it."

She shows it to me, and I almost cry.

"I'll keep it until you get a computer so you can download it."

"Thank you, that's very kind. Where is Judy?"

"She called a couple of hours ago asking if we could watch Mariah. She said she had a doctor's appointment, and the boys both had plans, so we said yes. I hope you don't mind."

"If she would've told me, I'd have taken off early and come home. I feel bad that she called you. Is she okay? That's her second doctor appointment this week. That's unusual for her, isn't it?"

"She didn't tell me she had another one. In fact, she didn't say what this was for, just that she and Dad were going to dinner when they were done. That's weird. I'll have to ask her tomorrow. Listen, I've wanted to talk to you for a while and wasn't sure how to approach you. Do you have a few minutes? I won't take much of your time."

I'm still not sure how to be rude to this woman so I just say, "Okay," and sit down on the couch placing the baby back on the floor. I cross my arms in front of me and sort of hunch over, almost like I'm protecting myself from her. A psychologist would have a field day with my body language right now.

"First, let me say that I'm sorry for everything I said on Thanksgiving. I said a lot you probably aren't even aware of. I kind of had a mental breakdown that day. I love your daughter. She's a sweet little girl with a happy heart, and I've missed my time with her. When I lost my mind that day, I hadn't slept in over twenty-four hours and was apparently fighting pregnancy hormones I didn't know I had, which were kicking my ass. I'm pregnant. Almost four months along now." A huge smile spreads across her face.

I smile at her, I'm happy that she's getting what she's wanted for so long.

"Congratulations you two, that's fabulous. I understand about the pregnancy hormones. I was a mess, too, and every little thing made me cry a river. I was also dying of exhaustion. I get it."

"Well there's more to it than that, and I'd like to explain."

"You don't have to."

"I realize that, but I want to. Bobby and I started dating in college and have been together now for over ten years. I've never looked at another man since we've been together. In my family, cheating wasn't acceptable. I never even thought about cheaters past what you see on television shows. My parents set the tone, and that's just how it was, until it wasn't anymore.

"Matt was my favorite brother and one of my closest friends. I looked up to him, thought he was so great. He spoiled me and treated me like a princess. In high school, he beat up guys who treated me like crap and shunned the girls who acted like bitches to me. He helped with my math and shot hoops with me after dark when I was trying to make the basketball team.

"He was loyal, sweet, funny, caring, and helpful. When he died, I shut down. I've never felt anything worse in my life. I must have carried my depression into the depths of my marriage, because my husband said I started acting different. I was short tempered, rude, and lazy. I stopped doing stuff around the house. I just left it for him to do. We were trying to get pregnant, so I only had sex on a schedule. With every failed attempt, I got meaner.

"When Lisa showed up and told us about you and Mariah, I hit rock bottom. I kind of lost it for a while. You saw for yourself that I was a snarky bitch. I was rude and condescending, not just to Bobby, but to everyone. We were still only having sex on the schedule according to the ovulation predictor, so I started to accuse Bobby of sleeping around.

"In my head, if Matt the Almighty could be a cheater, then anyone could. I thought Bobby's lack of interest in sex was because he was getting it elsewhere when in all actuality, it was because I'd set it up that way and left no room for discussion. It didn't help that I was a raging bitch to him. I was checking his texts, call logs, and voice mails. I even followed him one night when he went out with the guys. It was the most boring four hours of my life.

"When I had my blow up that day with you, my dad called me on my shit. He said I needed to work out my problems at home and quit using everyone else as a punching bag. Bobby took me home that night, and we had a long talk. We started couples counseling that next week, and I also started individual counseling. I had a lot to deal with. I still do. I also found out the same week I was pregnant. I just didn't tell anyone right away because I was afraid I'd lose it.

"Since starting counseling, I've realized I was blaming you for Matt's shortcomings so I wouldn't have to blame him. I've been really angry with him for everything he's done to Lisa, to you, to the other women. I'm pissed that he's dead, and I can never confront him and, sadly, at the same time I still miss him.

"So, I wanted you to know that I am sorry from the bottom of my soul for everything. You have been nothing but amazing to my family, and you filled a hole for all of us by coming here with Mariah. We all needed that even if none of us realized it right away. I hope you can forgive me. If you can't, I understand. I also want you to know that Bobby and I would love to watch her whenever you need us to. We've both missed her. She's so much fun."

A stray tear runs down the side of my face, and I smile at her. As much as I want to remain mad at her, I know it's not the right thing to do. "I get it and I do forgive you. If the situation were reversed, I don't know how I would act so don't worry about it. We just move on from here."

A bright smile spreads across her face, and she hugs me. Then Mariah and I pack up and leave.

All weekend, I worry about Judy. I know something is wrong, and I hate not knowing what's going on. On Sunday, I go to get dressed and realize I have nothing that fits right. It's all about a size too big. I have to go shopping, if nothing else for clothes to wear to work this week. I haven't felt like eating much, and it's starting to show.

I drive over to Target and get several outfits to get

me through the week. I figure I'll go shopping again after the next paycheck and just make this stuff work. As I'm getting Mariah back into the car, my phone rings. I pull it out of my purse and answer without looking at the caller I.D.

"Hello?"

"It's Johnny."

"Um. Hi. I'm just getting into the car. What can I help you with?"

"Mom has called a family dinner tonight." I'm not sure what that has to do with me unless they want Mariah there.

"I can drop Mariah off for you if you'd like."

"No. We want you both here, but Mom specifically asked for you."

"Why? What's going on?" I think he's full of crap.

"Because you're family, and she has something she wants to talk to all of us about at the same time, I guess."

"I'm not family, but if she wants me there, I'll be there."

"You *are* family." His voice is hard. His words are firm. "I'll see you soon. She wants us all there as soon as everyone can come."

"Okay, I'll head that way."

"See you soon."

"Yeah, see you."

I hang up and head over to the Brownings' home, wondering what in the world she'd want me there for.

Chapter Seven

Johnny

I have a bad feeling about this 'family dinner' Mom has called. It's been a long time since we had one. After the last one, we found out about Jill and Mariah's existence. Required family dinners always mean bad news, and something tells me this is going to be a doozie.

When I pull in the driveway, I see that both Steve and Bobby's vehicles are already here. Jill pulls in right behind me as I'm climbing out, so I lean into the back seat, take Mariah out of her car seat, and nuzzle her neck. She giggles and squirms to get down, so I hold tight and follow Jill inside.

We greet everyone and are hustled to the dinner table. My dad says, "Let's have a nice dinner, and we can talk afterward."

We all watch each other cautiously. Jill may not know the particulars of these kinds of dinners, but she's been around enough to know that whatever is coming won't be good.

After dinner, Dad sends us all to the family room and tells us we can clean the dinner dishes later. That never happens. On a normal night, Mom likes to get it out of the way right away. She's been unusually quiet tonight. Right now, she's sitting on the love seat next to my dad whose arm drapes protectively around her shoulders, with Mariah standing between her legs holding on. It's a new trick of hers, and she grins her four-tooth grin at everyone as they clap when she pulls herself up. Bobby is in the recliner with Tara on his lap. Steve and Mary are on the couch, his arm around her while she leans on him. Jill is on the floor sitting cross-legged next to a basket of toys. I'm on the other side of the basket with my legs stretched out in front of me.

My dad clears his throat and adjusts his body so Mom can lean into him a little and says, "Your mom and I have been to the doctor a couple of times this week and once last week. We didn't want to alarm you in case it was nothing, but we now have all the information."

Mariah is banging her little baby fist on Mom's leg trying to get her attention, so Jill leans in and pulls her back by us in an attempt to switch her focus to the basket of toys.

"Your mother has breast cancer, but they won't be able to stage it until after the surgery."

Silence blankets the room. Mariah even seems to have gotten the memo. All eyes are on Dad waiting for him to finish.

"She has to have a mastectomy and has opted to have it in both breasts since the reoccurrence possibility is so high. She'll have to have both radiation and chemo. We won't know the particulars on those parts until the surgery is completed, and she is cleared to begin. She's already had a consult with the surgeon, the oncologist, and the radiologist. The surgery is scheduled for next week. I know that doesn't give you all much time to absorb the information, but everything we've researched says the sooner she does this, the better."

I swallow hard. It feels like I'm trying to get a boulder down my throat. My eyes sting as I battle back the tears that threaten to fall. I try never to cry in front of my mother or anyone for that matter, but especially my mother. Jill must notice my reaction because the toy basket is moved from between us, and she scoots next to me, placing her hand over mine, and dragging them both into her lap.

Tara is the first to ask, "Oh, Mom. Why didn't you tell us something was going on?"

My mom lifts sad eyes to Tara.

"I was scared. I didn't want to upset you until I had to. You all have been through enough in the last year and a half without adding this. I knew I'd tell you eventually, but I needed to get all of the information first. It's going to be okay; it's just going to be a tough row to hoe. I'm going to need all of your help to get through this."

Jill has my hand in a death grip, and I think she's trying not to lose it also. This will change a lot for her again, and I really think she cares about my mom. They seem to spend a lot of time together.

I speak up, "Whatever you need, Mom. I'll be glad to help. I can take off as much time as I need. I'll work on hiring temporary help so I'm more available. What do you need from us right now?"

My mom's lip quivers, and I can see her hands are shaking a little. My dad must notice because he speaks for her, "I've put in for FMLA at work, and it's been granted. Luckily, I have four weeks of vacation time on the books that will be used first, so I'll get a paycheck for a month. Your mom is taking medical leave, and

I'm trying to talk her into retiring altogether so she doesn't have to go back once she feels better.

"I'll be around to take her to appointments and all of that, but I could use some help around here. We all know I'm a terrible cook unless it's on the grill, and it's still too damn cold to grill right now. As other things come up, we will let you know. The biggest thing your mom is worried about is Mariah."

Jill releases my hand and starts to gesture wildly, panic lacing her voice as she speaks.

"No, no, no! Don't worry about her. I'll figure something out with work and will hire someone to get her from daycare, or I'll see if I can find a daycare open later. Please don't worry about her. We will work it out. I just want Judy to get better. I promise we'll be okay."

Her voice breaks on the last word, and I pull her into my chest as she unleashes the tears.

My dad speaks up in a gruff voice and says, "Jill, I know you'd take care of that on your own. You've always been willing to find a way, but to be honest, there are enough of us that we should be able to handle this in the family. The thought of Mariah being with someone other than family any more than she has to be doesn't sit well with me. Part of the reason she's so happy is because she knows she's loved with all of us. I know we aren't perfect, but you've got to admit the nine of us make a nice family." He gives her a gentle smile. "Don't you think?"

Mary speaks next. "Steve and I can take turns picking her up and help out here, too. Don't worry about that at all. That is the easy part. We're all here for each other."

She reaches across the couch and grasps my mom's

hand. Steve hasn't said a word. He nodded when Mary spoke but has been staring off into space ever since.

Tara kneels in front of Mom on her knees, wraps her arms around her waist, and cries.

"It's going to be okay, Mom. We will all take care of you, Dad, and each other. You just have to tell us what you need when you need it. Let us worry about the rest, okay?"

We spend the next hour talking to each other and asking questions. After that, everyone leaves. I stick around to clean up dinner, and when I'm done I leave my parents' house, not quite ready to go home, so I drive around town to clear my head and to process what I've just been told.

At the end of my drive, I'm sitting in front of Jill's apartment. I know I should drive away. We've already caused each other so much pain, but I need her, and I have a feeling she needs me, too. I jump out of the truck and make my way to her front door knocking softly, praying she'll hear it, and at the same time, scared to death she will.

It takes me knocking a second time before she answers. The look on my face must convey what I'm feeling, because she doesn't even question my presence at her place. She opens the door wider and steps to the side, gesturing for me to come in.

I walk through the door stopping just inside, unsure of what to say exactly. Her place smells like baby lotion and gingerbread candles. Jill's in a pair of those casual, but sexy, ass-hugging yoga pants and a long sleeve t-shirt. It's obvious she's not wearing a bra by the natural curve of her breast evident against the cotton. Her dark hair hangs softly down her back. Her face has been scrubbed of all traces of makeup, and the little freckles that sprinkle her nose are visible. She's so damn beautiful that my body reacts in an instant. I should be ashamed that I can't control myself, but I'm not sure I would if I could. There is just something about her.

When she locks the door behind me, she says, "Go on in and have a seat. Want anything to drink?"

I shake my head no and run my hands through my hair in a 'what the hell am I doing here' kind of gesture as I make my way to the couch. I sit down on the edge with my elbows on my knees and my hands hanging loosely between my legs. I must look like hell because she sits down next to me and puts her hand on my back in a comforting manner and asks, "Are you okay?"

I know my eyes convey everything I'm feeling— sad, angry, and mixed-up—because her face softens as she studies me and she touches my cheek with the backs of her fingers tenderly.

"Why did you come here tonight, Johnny?"

She returns her hand to her lap and watches me like she's trying to figure me out. Her body language is relaxed. It hasn't been like this with us since before Thanksgiving, and I've missed it. Missed her. Her face is carefully blank as she asks, and I wish she'd show me something. Anything. I don't want to mess things up again, but I want her more now than before, like I've wanted no one else, ever.

I take a deep breath and exhale, never breaking eye contact.

"I wanted to be with you; in any capacity you'll let me."

"I'm sure you could have gone to Mindy or any number of women. Why here? Why me?"

"Because I'm in love with you. You know that. I have been since the first damn day in Indy. I want you so bad it hurts, but if friendship is all you have for me, I'll accept it. There's just something about you that makes my life better, and after everything tonight, I needed better. I've missed you."

Her lips part, and the surprise is evident on her face.

"You don't have to lie to me for comfort, Johnny. I'll be your friend without the pretty words."

"They aren't pretty words, honey. I told you how I felt before. That hasn't changed. It's the truth. I only went out to the bar and met Mindy because I was lonely, and you said you only wanted to be friends. I broke up with her before I was here the last time. She's not the one I want. I haven't been with anyone else. I don't want anyone else. I wanted more with you. I still want more, but like I said, I'll take what you're willing to give."

****

Jill

Without another word, I crawl into his lap. It's probably wrong for me to be doing this, but like him, I want the comfort of his arms. I need the intimacy. This is the closest thing to a real family I've ever had and in the months since I've been here, I've grown to love John and Judy. What Judy is facing is horrible and threatens to bring my happy family to its knees. I'm not ready to watch her suffer as she fights or to possibly lose her in the end.

We stay quiet like this for a long time, and I know I should let him go, but I'm feeling selfish and can't end it before he does. The sound of his heart beating in his chest, the warmth I feel in his strong, comforting arms, and the peace I have just resting with him is new for me. Even when I was with Matt, I never had peace. I was happy until the end with him, but I never felt this little slice of calm. At some point, I must have dozed off because I wake up to realize that I'm being carried to my room. He lays me down and starts to cover me up, and I do the second stupidest thing I've ever done; I beg him to stay. At first, he declines.

"I need you, Johnny. Please stay with me."

I can tell the moment he relents. His body relaxes, and his eyes lock with mine as he removes his shirt, jeans, socks, and shoes, leaving on only his tight, black, boxer briefs.

He's a big guy with the clothes on, but when his clothes come off, he is all manly fucking man. More man than I've ever seen, at least this close up. I love his rugged mechanic's hands that are all calloused and scarred. The swirling black tribal tattoos that stretch from his muscled forearms, over his broad shoulders and across his defined pectoral muscles lead my eyes along the landscape of his body. His toned and tight abs alone could bring me to my knees, along with his powerful shapely legs and a bulge in his boxers that I've dreamed about every night since he was last in my bed. The room is dark with slivers of moonlight that crisscross his body. There's a sudden flutter in my chest and a burning in my loins.

I'm not wearing a bra under my shirt, and I can feel my nipples, erect with desire, poking into the fabric. I shuffle the yoga pants down my legs and toss them to the floor as I scoot over so he can join me. I just wanted some comfort from his arms tonight, but the minute I got a glimpse of his body again, my wants became a whole lot more grown up. I try to tamp down my reaction to him. It's not fair for me to say we can't be together and then jump him the minute he's close to me. I lift up the sheet for him and he slips in to spoon up behind me wrapping his arm around my waist and connecting our bodies from my shoulder blades to our feet.

He's not in this position long before I feel his erection grow between us. It's hard and long against my behind, and it's all I can do to stifle the groan that threatens to escape my throat. My heart is hammering in my chest and my thighs clench together as I fight to keep my breathing even. I'm afraid he can hear it. He hasn't moved. In fact, he's holding deathly still.

"What's wrong, Johnny?"

"I'm trying to get myself under control. I'm not ready to leave. I know sex is out of the question, so I don't want to freak you out."

"You're not freaking me out. I'm having a hard time, too." I confess.

Obviously surprised he asks, "You are?"

"Yes," I answer and flex my hips into him.

He squeezes my waist with his arm and nuzzles the back of my neck. His breath sends goose bumps across my flesh. I lace our fingers together and slip them under my shirt to my straining breast. The vibration of his groan rumbles over me, and I flex our hands to squeeze. I twist my neck seeking his lips with mine, and his woodsy, clean scent washes over me and works like a potent aphrodisiac, turning me on even more.

He whispers into my ear, "What do you want, Jillian?"

"You."

"Are you sure? I can just go to sleep. I don't want you doing anything you don't want to do. I don't want to go there and have it turn out like it did last time. It almost killed me."

"I'm sure this is what I want."

I guess no further words are needed because he rolls me to my back, pulls my shirt up awkwardly over my head, and shoves it over the side of the bed. He's quick to shuffle his boxers off next.

"So damn sexy, woman," he rumbles over me and laces both hands into my hair, grasping the back of my head and pulling me toward his waiting mouth. His words spark an instant frenzy. Our mouths crush together in crazed excitement, all tongues and teeth.

He shifts to his back so I'm on top, and his hands explore my breasts, his thumb and forefingers roll my nipples as he commands, "Look at me."

My eyes comply immediately.

"I want you thinking of no one but me as I fuck you, Jill."

Seeking the necessary friction, I wiggle and reply, "There is no one else but you, Johnny."

"Good, because I won't share you, even with a memory." He growls out. "I want to watch you come. I want to see your face while I fill you. I don't want to miss a single second of this."

Holy shit. That's hot! I've never been with a dirty talker before. Never thought much about it, but I've got to say that it's doing it for me.

He rolls me to my back again, leans off the bed, flicks on the bedside lamp, and grabs a condom. Then he rolls it down over his thickness and contrary to the crazed way we tore at each other moments ago, he fills me with his enormous shaft in leisurely strokes. It takes me a little bit to acclimate to his size, but it feels so good. This is different from what we experienced the last time. The light is on, so I can see everything and somehow that makes what we are doing feel bigger and better than before.

"Are you okay, love?"

"Yes, yes, I'm perfect. So damn good." I tell him in a whisper.

"Can you take all of me? I'm not all the way in."

"Oh my God! Are you serious? I feel so full. Keep going. I want it. I want all of you."

He thrusts the rest of the way in, and I let out a shocked shriek. It's just this side of painful, but feels so, so, so good.

"God, that feels so good, Johnny." I moan.

He pumps his hips, pushing in and withdrawing, moving so slowly it's maddening, allowing my body to adjust each time. I lock my ankles behind his back and squeeze his ass cheeks with greedy hands when his hips are flush with mine. He groans, and I watch as the tension builds around his eyes. I can tell he's holding back, trying to last. I don't want that. I want him lost in the sensation, ravenous, and out of control so I squeeze my sex as tight as I can over and over, gripping him from within. I can literally see and feel when his control snaps. The tension pulls tight in every muscle as he crushes his mouth to mine and changes speed, pounding into me. His balls slap my ass with each thrust. He's groaning, and I gasp as he bottoms out. It's heaven and hell all mixed into one.

He pumps hard until he finally explodes inside of

me, the condom filling with his hot seed. His hips snap to mine for the last few strokes, draining every last drop. Euphoria hit me somewhere in the middle of it all, and I am more than halfway built up for more when he rolls off of me, disposes of the condom and drops back between my legs face first. I didn't realize he even knew I needed to come again. Crooking his fingers at the perfect angle inside me, he massages just the right spot. When he combines his lips and tongue, I get lost in the sensation until I'm screaming his name.

As I float back to Earth, completely spent, I lay here trying to find my breath as he moves up beside me and pulls me on top of him. My head is now on his chest, legs straddled on either side of his powerful hips and I can feel him smoothing my long hair back and out of the way. I'm a little shocked all of our noise didn't wake the baby, but I can still hear her soft snores through the monitor as she sleeps.

We are both sticky and smell of sex, but I don't care. I know when morning comes we'll have to go back to the way things were before, and I never want to go back there. I'm in love with Johnny, and he told me he feels the same. I've fought it and denied it, and tried to ignore it. I was having a hard enough time staying away from him before, but now that I know what's in his heart, and the kind of magic he can perform between the sheets, I'm not sure I can stay away. He is the complete and total package. Head to toe, inside and out, top to bottom, he's everything I've ever wanted in a man and thought I would never have.

I know he deserves someone better, someone who won't turn his world into an episode of Jerry Springer. I hate that I've brought that kind of drama into his life, but I'll be hard pressed to stay away from him now. After hearing Judy's news today, I'm reminded of how short life really is. Should I give into what I really want or continue to fight it? I know down in my heart I'm not what's best for Johnny and I hate it. I'm just not strong enough to stay away anymore.

I squeeze my arms around his torso and grip his waist with my knees. I don't want to let go. I'm afraid when I do, this little fantasy will be over and I'll be back to my exhausting, lonely life.

His voice is masculine and gravelly as he says, "You're so beautiful. Perfect almost. Every curve, every line, perfect, but I have to ask why you've lost so much weight?"

"I don't want to talk about it. It's not something I'm comfortable with."

"I don't care, Jill. I've got you here in my arms, and there are things we need to talk about and that's a big one."

"Why do we need to talk about it? Why can't we just stay like this and pretend everything is okay?"

"Because I care about you, Jill, and I know as soon as we get dressed you're going to lock me out again. I want to know what's going on."

I huff out an irritated breath and try to roll off him, but he grips me harder and pleads, "No way. Stay where you are. Just talk to me, please."

"I haven't been eating much, that's all."

"Do you have food? Do you need money?"

"No, I have plenty, it's not that. Please don't make me say this."

"Tell me, Jill."

"When I get depressed, I don't eat. When I try to, it

makes my stomach upset, so I just don't. Well, not much anyway. I try a little, for Mariah's sake. I haven't lost much this time only ten pounds or so."

"Oh God, Jill. You didn't have that to lose. I love your body, but you've lost too much and I'm worried. Why are you depressed?"

I shake my head, not wanting to answer. Confessing your innermost demons is painful.

"Jillian." It isn't just my name on his lips, it's a warning. I know I'm not getting out of this bed without answering so I suck up the fear and share the truth.

"I was upset about things with us. Seeing you with Mindy. The last fight we had. Tara. Lisa. How stupid I am in general. How damn stupid I am with the choices I make in life."

His arms tighten around me.

"Jill. I never meant to hurt you that night. I was so jealous. So pissed you wouldn't go out with me, but you let that douchebag kiss you and I saw it. I've wanted you for so long, and all you could give me was excuses. Then, when you finally let me in, I thought it was going to be okay, so I was shocked when you ended up throwing me out. I want this, Jill. I want there to be an us. I want both you and Mariah. I don't want to help raise her as my niece; I want to raise her as my daughter. I want it all with you. You've been losing weight because of the things I said to you?"

A tear slides out of my eye as I answer.

"It's not just what you said. It's knowing that I'll never be good enough. Not for you or anyone else. It's the pain of knowing no one loves me, and I don't deserve to be loved. If my own parents couldn't love me, I don't know why I ever thought anyone else would. It's because I constantly screw things up in my life without even realizing it. I just want a happy life. I don't need money or material things. I just want to love and be loved. I want to take care of the people I care for, and I want to be worthy of that."

The tears that start at the beginning of my confession get progressively worse and flow so hard I can't breathe. Moving both hands up over the skin of my back, along the curve of my shoulders, and under my hair to my jaw line, he lifts my face to his so I can see his eyes as he talks to me.

"Jill, please let me love you. I'm nothing like Matt or any of the idiots you've dated. I'm nothing like your parents either. I just want to be with you. I already love you for who you are. You make mistakes. I make mistakes, too. It's part of being human. You've got to let go of the voices of your past and listen to the voice of your future. I. Love. You. Just the way you are. You're an amazing mother, a hard worker, thoughtful and incredibly beautiful. In my eyes, you're perfect. I need you to believe me, to give me a chance. I've missed you so much."

"What about Mindy?"

"I already told you I broke up with her. She was a place-filler. I thought if I was distracted that I wouldn't want you so much, but I was wrong. I broke up with her for that reason. I knew it was only you I wanted."

"Then why did you bring her to your parents' house? Everyone said you hadn't brought anyone home with you in years. I was certain you'd marry her. When I saw her with you at the mall, I wanted to die and then I had to see you with her at your mom's house and it was pure torture."

"She invited herself, to be honest. She heard me talking to Mom on the phone and just invited herself. When it didn't seem to matter to anyone, I went ahead and let her do it again. I didn't think you really cared."

I almost can't breathe thinking about everything he's said, so I turn my head to place a gentle kiss on his chest and then put my cheek back down where it was. I run my fingers through the little bit of chest hair he has, scraping my nails softly on his skin. I apply a kiss to each of his nipples and a little lick. Then I lift my head to kiss his soft lips. I put all of my wishes and wants for him into that one kiss. I can feel him harden between us again and without thinking, I move my body until I can slip him inside me. He fills me almost to bursting. So damn big and thick that I'm a little afraid he might split me down the middle, but so damn good. He lets out a strangled sound as I lift and lower on him, again and again.

"Oh God, you feel so fucking good, Jill. Oh, fuck. Don't stop," he grinds out between clenched teeth.

I continue to lift and lower, moving as slowly as I can, grinding my hips on the down stroke, hitting my clit just right every single time. His hands are on my breasts pinching and twisting my nipples, drawing whimpers from my lips.

I think he finally has enough of my slow, sensual assault because he flips me so my back hits the sheets, then he rolls me to my stomach. Yanking my hips up, he braces himself behind me and thrusts in, doggie style. It's so deep like this, and he seems to be hitting that special spot hidden deep within me. I'm drowning in the sensations pouring over me. After several strokes, he pauses. I turn my head to look back at him, ready to beg him to keep going if I have to.

"What's wrong?"

"I'm not wearing a condom. I just realized it. I don't have another one. Do you have any?"

"Um…No. I haven't been with anyone to need them, but I'm on the pill."

"Okay, honey."

I twist farther so I can see his expression, and his giant hand cups my chin as he bends down to kiss me. It's tender and sweet and something I never want to live without. His lips move from my lips to graze my shoulder blades and then withdraw altogether.

I almost cry out in relief when he slides his cock back inside me. His strong fingers grip my hips as he sets a punishing rhythm. I drop my chest to the bed and arch my back so he's as deep inside of me as he can go. So big and so hard, working furiously, he finds that spot again, the one that blurs the line between pleasure and pain. My body shatters again as the force of my orgasm barrels though me. I'm delirious in post orgasmic bliss as he rolls me to my back and kisses his way from my lips down over the sensitive tips of my breasts. Then he continues lower over the pouch that still hasn't disappeared from carrying the baby, until he reaches the lips of my sex. I'm so hypersensitive that my whole body comes off the bed at first contact.

This is an area I've decided he excels in. He knows exactly what to lick, lave, suck, and stimulate and exactly what to avoid. His special attention leaves me convulsing as my body explodes once more. He moves back up my body placing his mouth on mine. I can still smell and taste my tangy cream on his lips, and I give him a sleepy smile of satisfaction.

I shift my weight and push him to his back so I can slither down between his legs. I lift his giant sack into my tiny hand and massage it gently. I watch his reaction to my every movement hoping to discover what he likes the best. Then I run my tongue up the seam in the middle all the way up his steely shaft and back down.

I'm careful as I suck his balls into my mouth, humming softly. I repeat the process over again making sure to cover all the skin. His sac draws up tighter to his body the more I work him. My hand slides slow controlled strokes over his cock while I give all of my oral attention to the tender, softer skin that hangs between his legs.

When I notice that his thigh muscles are rock hard and his body is vibrating, I turn my attention to the purple mushroom head of his cock. I slide my lips over and down taking as much of him as I can into my throat. My hand is working in tandem and he's thrusting into my mouth with short uncontrolled stokes. His eyes are glued to me, watching me take him in. I can feel his hands grip my hair tighter as his balls pull up more and I know it's coming. I've never swallowed before, but I want to try it so I go for it. I work him hard, ignoring his warnings, stealing his control, until he suddenly blows, spurting his hot, sticky liquid into the back of my throat.

The first shot is choking, but after that, it's okay so I continue to swallow and suck until there is nothing left. I let his flaccid cock slip from between my lips and I drop down on the pillow beside him.

We lay there in silence for a few minutes with him trying to catch his breath and me, thinking too hard and too much about things I can't control. I'm scared to hope, scared to act on this thing with him and scared to believe in the things he's promising me.

"You need to quit thinking so hard and just let me love you." His voice is still gruff with the remnants of our lovemaking.

I readjust myself to look at him and notice his hair is disheveled from my fingers tugging on the strands in the heat of the moment. I adore the just-sexed look of him, especially since I made him that way.

I search his face for inconsistencies, little signs that tell me he's not telling the truth, like maybe he doesn't really want there to be an us. After the nightmare with Matt, I'm terrified to believe what he has to say. There were so many nights that Matt told me things I later found to be lies. The reality of my life with Matt almost broke me. Thank goodness for Mariah or I may never have survived the absolute heartbreak.

His deep voice breaks the silence once again. "I'm nothing like him. I never was. I was the night to his day and the hot to his cold. He was my brother, and I loved him, but we were never anything alike."

My eyes snap to his, and I wonder how he could know what I was thinking.

Calloused fingers sift into my hair and hold my face still, his hovers just above mine now. "I've been honest with you from the start. You know how I feel about you. I'll say it over and over if you need to hear it, but I need to know how you feel about me. I've put myself out there and it's a scary place to be alone."

"I'm afraid. I can't seem to break away from that feeling," I confess.

"I know you are. I am, too, but I'm willing to try.

Are you? Don't you see we are so much better together than alone?"

His emerald eyes hold mine as he waits for my response. He's vulnerable right now, in every way possible and it's probably the sexiest thing I've ever seen in my life.

Keeping my eyes on his, I decide to leap right over the edge with him.

My voice is quiet as I tell him, "I love you, too. I have for a long time now. I love your strength and your ability to find softness for me. I love how you are with your family. I love how you just tell it like it is; there is never any hidden meaning in your words. I love that you love Mariah and were sneaking over to see her when we weren't talking. I love how you treat your mom and dad. I love that you're big enough to hold me on your lap and protect me from the world. I love that you didn't get a suit-and-tie job like your brothers, but instead opened your own shop and still work under the hood of a car every day.

"I love that you fixed my tires and stayed at the bar that night to make sure I was okay. I love that you beat that guy up for hitting me. I love that I'm lying here with the sexiest man I've ever seen, and he's not afraid to tell me that he loves me for who I am. I love that my sheets will now smell like you until I make myself wash them. I love that every time I walk past this bed I'm going to think of our time making love here."

I kiss his lips as if to punctuate the words and put my head back to the pillow. He studies my face for a few brief moments before his lips descend to mine. For the next hour, he makes slow, sweet love to every inch of my body, the whole time telling me everything that he loves about me. It's absolute heaven.

****

My body jolts, and my eyes blink open at the sound of the alarm. I roll over to look at the clock as I turn it off. I'm exhausted, but strangely happy. My body is achy in a good I'm-all-sexed-up sort of way. I only got a couple of hours of sleep and none of them in a row. I also woke up next to Johnny, which I've decided could make even the worst morning awesome.

As I'm about to crawl out of bed, his gruff morning voice says, "Stay with me a little bit longer. I will take Mariah to day care after I check in with Mom and Dad. It will give me some time with her and a little more time with you this morning. Okay?"

"Well, who is going to argue with that? Not me!"

I giggle as he pulls me back across the bed and tucks me into the crook of his arm, leaving my head to rest on his chest and my fingers to trace the patterns of ink on his skin. He kisses the top of my head and slides his hands over my naked skin, anywhere he can reach.

"Are you going to have dinner with me tonight? I'll cook."

I lift up on an elbow to make eye contact. I'm not able to keep the skepticism from my voice when I ask, "You can cook? We're not talking take out on plates at home, right? Like real food cooked by your hands?"

He flips me to my back and tickles me until I'm squealing and squirming.

"You doubt my domestic prowess?"

He nuzzles my neck right before he nips at the tender skin, and softly licks over the sting.

"No, never, well, maybe a little…"

I can't hide the smile that stretches across my face.

The tickles restart, and I squeal again. Before I can fully recover, his hips shift, and he's grinding at a slow, maddening pace to work his way fully inside me. I gasp at the odd pleasure as he stretches the sore places left over from last night's activities and wrap my legs around him.

His gaze burns into mine as he rolls his sexy hips, driving inside me deeper each time. His arm muscles flex above me as I run my fingers over every one of them. I pull his beautiful scruffy face to mine and kiss him like I need to eat him, biting his lower lip, sucking on his tongue and holding him to me with my hands on the back of his head.

My body arches up to meet his, and my moans grow in volume and strength until a brilliant light explodes behind my eyes as I find the happiest of happy places. He continues to hammer into me like a madman on a mission, until I feel him erupt within me. The hot rush of his semen and the weight of his body as he finishes alerts me to the fact that we didn't use protection this time, and I panic.

I'm on the pill, but in the light of day, I am afraid anyway, especially since we went without last night. I'm obviously "Fertile Myrtle," and the chances that I'd get pregnant are huge. I don't want him to think I'm trying to trap him, too. I push with my hands and try to scramble out from under him, but he holds me there with his weight and the position of his body over mine.

"Don't freak out, Jilli. I realized it too late, and I know why you're freaking out. It wouldn't be ideal timing, but I can't say that I'd be unhappy if you had my baby growing inside of you. I meant what I said about loving you and wanting a life with you. If you'd let me marry you tomorrow, I'd do it. If you'd move in with me tomorrow, I'd pack you up today. I'll be more careful in the future, but you don't have to worry about the same thing with me, okay? I promise."

As if to emphasize his point, he kisses me slowly, sweetly, and tenderly. Then he rolls away and says, "You'd better get ready for work. I can hear Mariah squawking, so I'll go get her up and changed. I'll see you in a few minutes."

I get one more kiss on the forehead, and he gets out of bed yanking up his jeans commando style as he leaves the room.

I lay there for a second trying to absorb everything he said in the last several hours. I realize at some point during the night, I must have fallen into the rabbit hole and should be seeing Alice in Wonderland any minute. That's how bizarre this all feels to me.

Now that I can hear the monitor clearly, Johnny's voice is loud and clear talking to Mariah.

"How's my baby girl this morning? I missed you."

Loud kissing and raspberries float through the air and wonderful little baby giggles follow. I take a shower knowing he has this taken care of.

Ready for work half an hour later, I tiptoe into the kitchen to spy on Johnny and Mariah. He's feeding her, and it's in her hair, on her face, and up her nose. She's having a blast with it this morning. He's still shirtless, wearing only his jeans with his bare feet tucked under the chair. All of his attention is on the baby as I observe their interaction. This is exactly what I wanted in my life. A sexy beast of a man in my bed at night who means it when he tells me he loves me and a soft soul who'll feed my little girl and chat her up first thing in

155

the morning.

I can feel the tears and the fear well up within me at this revelation. I feel so lucky at this moment to have everything I've ever wanted, but the ugly fear is seeping into my heart, leaving me scared to have it all disappear.

I'm still standing there lost in thought when Mariah calls out "Mamamamamama!"

Johnny's head whips around, and he must catch the look on my face before I can wipe it blank because he stands, wipes the food off his hands, and strides over to me. He grabs my face and kisses me hard.

"Don't overthink this, Jilli. This is the way it's meant to be. Okay?"

"Okay, I'll try. I'm just afraid."

"I know, honey, but it'll be okay. Just try to trust this. Trust us."

"I will, I'll try."

He kisses me gently this time as Mariah yells out again.

"Mamamamamamama!"

It dawns on me that this is the first time she's done that and been looking at me. She knows I'm her Mama. So awesome. I sneak over and get a face-full-of-food kiss and help to clean her up so I can hug her before I leave. Baby cuddles are the best.

****

A week goes by and the relationship building between Johnny and me is like nothing I've ever known. It's comfortable in a way that no relationship ever has been for me. I always equated comfortable with boring, but Johnny has made sure that's not the case. We haven't said anything to his family but decided that Sunday dinner tomorrow is when we will make the announcement. I'm nervous it's going to blow up on us and cause more stress for the family. He's arguing that his mom has her surgery on Monday, and he doesn't want the stress of trying to hide how he feels during all of this. I understand what he's saying and decide to follow his lead.

Mary already knows about the relationship with Johnny since I talk to her almost every day on my way home from work. Her friendship has been invaluable to me over the last couple of months. If Mary knows, I can assume Steve knows. He's not been my concern. The big concerns are his parents and Tara. I don't think Bobby cares one way or the other as long as Tara's happy, but history has shown that she's not been very receptive to anything concerning me. Sure, things have been better between us, but I'm not sure they will ever be great.

Sunday arrives, and I'm tired and nervous. I didn't sleep well last night. Mariah must sense my mood because she's been fussier than normal, and Johnny has had to bounce her in his arms for a good part of the morning. We ride over to his parents' house together. When we arrive, Tara is in the kitchen cooking, and his mom and dad are nowhere to be found.

Chapter Eight

Johnny

"Where are Mom and Dad?" I ask as I kiss Tara's cheek in greeting.

"Mom is lying down. She's been really tired. I sent Dad to check on her a few minutes ago, and he hasn't come back yet."

"How are you feeling, little sister? You look amazing."

"I'm good. Not as tired anymore. Just worried about Mom. We need to talk about a schedule to help Dad. I thought maybe after dinner, we could figure all of that out. I wonder if Mary and Steve are still okay picking up Mariah every day and keeping her until Jill gets home. Where are they by the way? I swear I heard someone come in with you."

"Jill and the baby are with me. Mariah has been fussy today, so Jill is trying to find something to keep her occupied."

"Sooooo, what's going on with you and Jill?"

In this moment, she doesn't sound like a bitchy little sister. She sounds like my ten-year-old sister teasing me because I like a girl, so I provide her with the requisite squinty-eyed glare.

"Well? Come on big brother! Spill the beans." She's smiling at me, and I realize how long it's been since I've seen her smile like this. I've missed it.

"We planned on telling everyone today after dinner. We're seeing each other."

"Thank God! I thought for sure we'd be stuck with that Mindy chick forever. Jill's a good choice. She fits in with all of us. She's got a cute kid. She loves Mom and Dad, and she's stupid in love with your ass."

My jaw practically hits the floor.

"What?"

"You heard me. I know you don't think I like her, but therapy has done wonders for me. I've come to realize that she is a good person. I don't think I'll ever be able to talk about Matt with her, but I do like her, and I think she's a good match for you. You complement each other well."

"Well, damn. I wish Jill had heard all of that. I think she's most concerned about your reaction, well, me too, if I'm being honest. After what Dad said on Thanksgiving, I think they will be okay."

"I think you're right."

The smile she returns spans the width of her face making it obvious she's happy for me.

I finish helping Tara prepare dinner right as Jill comes through the kitchen door. I turn, scoop her into my arms, and kiss her like I'm trying to remove her socks through her mouth. When I pull away, she's wild-eyed and breathless.

"What are you doing?" she whispers.

"Claiming my woman," I tell her with a shit-eating grin.

Her eyes are huge in her face right now, and I can't do anything but laugh.

Tara pipes up from behind me, "He already told me. Don't worry about it. I'm happy for you both, and I know you'll take care of each other. Once I got over being a bitch, I decided you two would make a great couple if you guys could figure your shit out. Oh yeah, and I didn't like Mindy. She was nice, but way overboard and a little pushy, too. If she were my sister-in-law, I'd have to slit my wrists or move to Japan. It would depend on my mood that day which choice I'd make."

Tara is being flippant in her remarks and hasn't looked up from what she was doing one time to notice Jill's shiny eyes, a clear indication that she's about to cry. I pull her into my arms and hold her close until she can reign in her emotions.

When she's finally calm, she leans around me and says, "Thanks, Tara. It really means a lot to me that you're okay with this. Oh, and I'm super glad you didn't like Mindy either. I was ready to have a cat fight with that woman at a family dinner for feeding him from her fingers."

Tara busts up laughing, and Jill follows suit. I'm standing there watching the two hyenas bark their laughter, trying to figure out how I never noticed that my family didn't like Mindy.

Mariah went down for an unscheduled nap, and the three of us set the table and got drinks. Once Steve and Mary arrive, we all sit down to dinner together. It turns out that Mom wasn't resting once Dad went in there. There are some things I hope I never have to see again, and one of them is my parent's making out like teenagers in their bed, half dressed with the door open. I guess I should be thankful they are still doing that kind of stuff, but if I never see it again, it'll be too soon.

At the end of dinner, Steve and Mary clean the

kitchen while the rest of us sit and talk. I fill Mom and Dad in on things with Jill, and the whole time I'm talking, her hands are shaking and sweating. She's terrified.

"Well, it's about time, Son. Your mother and I have been watching this stupid dance you two have been doing since the day we moved her here. I could have saved you a lot of trouble by telling you to just go for it, but I knew you had to figure it out on your own. Let me just say, Mindy was a friendly girl, but if she never shows up here again I'll die a happy man." He chuckles as he finishes.

Exasperated, I ask, "Why didn't anyone tell me they didn't like her?"

My mom says, "Because you have to figure those things out on your own. We can't do it for you. I'm just glad you finally got smart and went after Jill."

"He did right before Thanksgiving, and I thought everyone would be upset, so I told him we should just be friends. Now I feel like an idiot."

"Don't. The timing wasn't right for one reason or another, and now it is. I'm just glad you two figured it out," my mother wisely states.

Jill leans in and gives me a small kiss, one that's appropriate in front of the family, and I grin at her.

****

Mom's surgery goes well, and we are all being sent home for the night. Jill left an hour ago to get Mariah and is meeting me at my house. We all took the day off from work, and everyone has to go back tomorrow except Dad and me, so we are going to take shifts with Mom until we can get relief in the evening. Our whole goal is to make sure that there is someone with her during the whole of visiting hours. It's going to be a long week.

****

Jill

Muddy puddles surround the driveway at Johnny's house. It rained most of the day while we were at the hospital, and the remnants are damp and dirty. I put Mariah on my hip, shoulder her diaper bag, and then attempt to drag in another bag filled with my stuff. As I juggle the bags and baby while trying to locate the keys, my bag falls to the ground dumping most of the contents on the wet, dirty cement. Yuck! I'm scrambling to gather it all up when Cici approaches.

"Let me help you. I saw you struggling over here, and I just couldn't get to you fast enough to catch any of it."

"Oh, it's okay. Thank you for your help. I didn't want to leave anything in the car and have to come back out while my daughter was in the house alone. I should have left it till Johnny came home."

"So are you and Johnny finally done dancing around each other?"

"Um…" I stare at her a little perplexed.

"I told you, our parents are close. They hear it all. Apparently, John and Judy have been waiting for you two to get together since you met. Johnny is a great guy. My Denton is without a doubt the best man around, but Johnny takes a close second."

"Denton?"

"That's my husband. We've been married for five years. I met him in college and made him come back to Cincy with me. He's a Texas boy, so he hasn't quite adjusted, but he will eventually. Let me help you inside with this stuff so your little sweetie doesn't freeze to death."

"Okay, I appreciate it."

"Mariah is a doll. She's cuter than the kids in the Anne Geddes pictures. I can't believe she got Matt and Steve's eyes though. That's got to sting a bit I bet."

"Um…yes, sometimes, but that was my favorite feature of Matt's so mostly no. I try to think of them as John Sr. and Steve's eyes. That helps."

Cici plops right down on the couch and makes herself comfortable. I'm not quite sure what to think of her yet. She's friendly and helpful, but she talks a lot. There is something about her though that makes me want to see what she might say next. It's kind of entertaining. I set Mariah down, and she army crawls her way over to the couch. She uses Cici's legs to pull herself to standing and proceeds to yell a bunch of baby babble at her and drool all over her jeans.

"I'm so sorry," I blurt out as I rush to move Mariah to a new location.

"Don't worry. I don't mind the slobbery little beast. I'm an artist and usually covered in all kind of things anyway. Well, I'm a vice detective by day at a precinct downtown and an artist the rest of the time. What do you do?"

"Nothing that exciting or fulfilling. I'm in the janitorial arts."

Her left eyebrow raises in question.

"It's a long story. I went to college for two years when I lived at home. I was three credit hours away from getting my AA when I decided to drop out. That is a story for another day, but I was a waitress at a dance club in Indy for several years. When I got too pregnant to do that anymore, I found a job as a janitor at a nursing home. When I moved here, the only job I could find that I was qualified for and didn't have me working third shift was a janitor position at an elementary school. It's a couple of blocks from Christ Hospital."

"That's a rough neighborhood, not far from my office."

"Yeah, it is, but it's a job with benefits and daytime weekday hours. Someday maybe I'll be able to go back to school. Right now, I'm still trying to survive."

"I understand. Hey, how's Judy? My mom told me she was having the surgery today."

"As good as can be expected. Surgery went well. We just have to wait to find out when they will start radiation and chemo. I was there with everyone today, but Mariah needed to be picked up, so I headed here before we were allowed to see her. Johnny didn't want to stay at my place tonight. He's complaining about his back and my crappy mattress, so I agreed to come here for a few nights. I just hate having to set up the pack 'n' play for her every time when she has a crib already up at my place."

"I don't think you're going to need the pack 'n' play."

"Why not?" I lift a brow, wondering what the heck she's talking about.

"Because I'm a hundred percent certain he has a regular crib in here already."

"What? Why would he have a crib here? Did Mindy have a kid?"

"No, that crazy bitch didn't have a kid. She was trying to have his though. She was pushing too hard, too fast, and it was obvious he wasn't quite as into her.

I watched as the crib was delivered last week during the day. He came home from work and met the delivery people to let them in. You didn't know?"

"No! He didn't say anything."

"That's just how he is, quietly thoughtful. When Denton was out of town a couple of years ago, my air conditioner broke, and I locked myself out of my house. It was a shitty day. Anyway, I came over here to use his phone, and when I told him what happened, he didn't say a word, just called an AC guy and a locksmith. Both showed up about the same time. He paid the locksmith before I could find my purse and did some kind of trade thing with the AC guy for work on his car. He never said a word, just did what needed to be done. He said if the roles were reversed, Denton would do the same for him. He probably would, but seriously, who does that for people?"

I get up out of the chair and wander back to the bedrooms. I haven't been anywhere in the house prior to this except the living room for a few minutes one time. The first bedroom has a queen-sized bed, a dresser, and a small desk. The second bedroom I come to is the master bedroom. It has zero in the way of decor, but it's spacious. A king-sized bed sits in the middle of the far wall; there is a tall dresser and a short wide dresser on opposite walls. There are also two bedside tables with lamps. On one of the bedside tables sits a picture of Mariah that someone took with a phone, I think. It's framed and dusty, so I know it's been there for a while. On the other side of the bed, there is another dust-covered frame. The picture is of the Browning clan when the kids were young. Johnny looks to be about eleven or twelve in the picture.

I set the picture back down and leave his room, entering the one across the hall and sure as shit I find a brand new crib with a pretty pink gingham sheet covering the mattress and a couple of brand new stuffed animals in it. There is also a matching dresser and changing table. My jaw hits the floor. He thought of everything.

I'm about to turn around to go back to Cici when she speaks from somewhere right behind me.

"He's a really good guy. I already knew that, but this just proves it."

All choked up, I can barely say, "Yeah, he really is."

I walk back to the living room with her and set Mariah on her feet on the floor. Cici excuses herself saying she'd love to get together sometime. I return the sentiment as she slips out the front door. Then I start the process of getting Mariah fed and bathed. I'm halfway through the bath when Johnny comes home. I look up to find him standing in the doorway watching as I work, with a soft expression on his tired face.

"How's your mom? Did you see her?"

"Yeah, we got to see her. She was out of it, but she smiled at us and said she felt groggy, and that was about it. It messed my dad up so much that he refused to leave her overnight. They are going to let him stay as long as he isn't disruptive. I plan to relieve him when visiting hours start tomorrow. The hospital has both of our phone numbers in case something changes during the night, so please keep your ringer on."

I finish rinsing Mariah, and Johnny shuffles over to the sink to grab the towel for her. Once I lift the wet baby into the air, he wraps the towel around her and pulls her into his arms. Her face lights up with happiness as soon as she touches his goatee, and the pulling begins. Smiling with obvious affection at her, he moves toward the bedroom to get her dressed. I place my hand on the tense muscles of his back following him out of the room and make a mental note to rub his back at bedtime.

"I can't believe you did all of this, Johnny." Palms up, I gesture around the room. "It was a very nice surprise today. You didn't have to."

"I know, but I wanted to. I wasn't kidding when I said I want it all with you, and until you'll let me give that to you, I want you both to be comfortable no matter where we spend our days or nights. You both deserve the best, and its time you started getting it."

I pass him the baby lotion and observe as he rubs her arms, legs, tummy, and then attempts her back, but gets a squirming, irritated baby instead of the cooperative one he's used to. He wrestles the diaper on her and picks her up, inhaling as he does. A soft happy groan escapes his throat as he holds her, and I watch as his body starts to shake. My man has hit his breaking point for the day.

I wrap my arms around the two of them the best that I can and wait for either the baby to lose patience or him to settle down. Baby patience wins, and I take her from him, tug a pair of fuzzy pink footie pajamas on her body, and lead them both out of the room to the couch. I place Mariah on the floor next to a basket of toys and drag Johnny down to the couch with me. He wipes his eyes and pulls me into his lap.

"I wish I could put you in my lap. Your lap is almost my favorite place in the world. I know it would help you."

His body shakes with a deep chuckle, and he squeezes tighter.

"This is good enough for me. It was so much easier for me to leave tonight, knowing you would be here when I got here."

"I'm glad we came then. By the way, Cici came in and chatted with me for a bit. She's interesting and very nice. She saw me dump all of my junk on the sidewalk trying to carry it all in at one time and came to help me. Then she stuck around for a bit and asked a hundred questions, before she told me she'd like to get together sometime. She said she's known your family most of her life. I actually met her when I came by to see you Thanksgiving Day. I just never got a chance to tell you."

"You came by before going to Mom's house?"

"Yes, I wanted to try to fix things with you. When you weren't here, I headed to your mom's house, and you know what happened after that. Anyway, that was the day I met her. She invited me out with her group of girlfriends, but she never called and things got so bad with you and me that I never asked you for her number."

"You'd probably like her friends. That girl is crazy, but she's sweet. Our families have been friends for years. Her brother is the same age as Steve and played little league with him, I think. She was always around. She and Steve were close during college. She moved in next door to me after she married Denton. She's always on question patrol and is fiercely protective of the people she cares about, but she'd give you the shirt off her back, if she thought it would help. Her husband's the same way. You'll like him. She just takes a little getting used to."

"She wasn't a fan of Mindy."

"I'm finding that no one was. I wish someone would have told me this at the time."

"I would have if I wasn't going to come off like a jealous shrew, but that would have been impossible. I was so jealous, I couldn't see straight." I give him a little grin.

The whole time we're talking, Mariah is holding onto the coffee table as she makes laps around it pulling off every magazine and coaster as she goes.

He leans in and whispers into my ear, "This is how things are supposed to be. I've got both of my girls in my house. One is in my arms while the other destroys the place. I love you, Jill. There is no place I'd rather be, and no one I'd rather be with."

"Me, too. I love you so much, and I really like your house. If your bed is as awesome as you say, I may not ever leave it."

"Don't make promises you don't intend to keep." He punctuates the sentence with a kiss on top of my head.

"Are you hungry? I can make you something before I put her to sleep."

"No, Dad and I got something to eat while Mom was still in recovery. Let's get Mariah to sleep and head to bed. I'm tired."

With all the lights out and the baby quiet, I give my man his back rub and take my time appreciating every last inch of his body. When I'm done, we fall asleep with me tucked in the crook of his arm, head on his chest, my arm stretched across his stomach.

****

The rest of the week passes in a blur of hospital visits, work, and trying to help Johnny keep it all together. Judy was expected out of the hospital on Thursday but got an infection in one of the drain sites, so she's in there until they can get that under control. She's been sore and grouchy, so we've been taking turns hanging out trying to keep her spirits up.

It's Saturday afternoon, and I'm sitting with Judy. I made everyone else take a few hours off. I hadn't been at the hospital all week except for a half hour every day on my lunch break because I had to work and pick up Mariah. I wanted to stay with her and I wanted to help, so Mary is watching the baby, and the guys took their dad to get lunch and kill time somewhere.

Judy's been asleep off and on all day, a side effect of the pain medication I'm sure. Flipping through the pages of a magazine one of the girls left behind, I'm too preoccupied to notice when someone steps into her room. A throat clears near the doorway, and I lift my head up to see who it is.

My breath catches in my throat as my eyes make contact with Lisa. I had no idea she was coming, and it's clear she had no idea I'd be here. I scramble out of my chair sending the magazine to the floor. Subtlety is not my strong suit.

My words are rushed, panicky as they leave my mouth, "I made everyone else take a break. They've been here all week. She's been in and out all day, but she'll be glad to see you. Just pat her hand, and she'll wake right up. I'll give you some time with her."

Even in my hurry to scurry past her, I notice the barely present baby bulge. I don't say a word. I don't want to upset her or Judy, so I scurry out the door. I'm met head on by a very attractive man. In fact, I smack right into him and he steadies me with his hands.

"Um. Hi. I'm sorry. I wasn't looking where I was going."

"Hi. Were you here with Mrs. Browning?"

"Yes."

"I'm here with Lisa. I'm Garrett." He puts his hand between us to shake.

"I'm Jill. I'm not family. I'm just trying to give them a break, they've been here all week around the clock."

"You're Jill?" His forehead wrinkles in confusion and then he wipes his face clean of expression.

"Yes."

I stare at the floor, ashamed. I know he knows who I am, and I'd love to have the floor swallow me up right now so I don't have to see the accusing eyes I'm certain are boring into me. I don't look up. I just start to shuffle past when he catches my arm. Startled, my eyes shoot up to his.

"It's okay. I'm not judging you, Jill. You're just not what I expected."

"After meeting Lisa, I bet not." I give an uncomfortable laugh.

"I didn't mean anything by that. You don't have to feel weird. She's moved on. We're together. She's having my baby." A huge smile spreads across his face. "She's due in June, and we're getting married in a few weeks, too."

I smile at him. "I'm happy for you both. Congratulations. She deserves to be happy."

"Yeah, she does."

"I'll let you go in there. I'm sure Judy is excited to meet you, but she's going to be mad that her hair isn't done."

He laughs a little and pauses to comment as he walks past. "You deserve to be happy, too. Sounds like life hasn't been easy on you, either. Try to let go of the past. She has."

"Thank you, I'm trying."

I share a small smile, and then I turn and walk away before things get awkward again.

I return half an hour later and sit on a chair outside of the room. I don't want to rush their time together, but I want to be near when they leave so Judy won't be alone. Twenty minutes later, Lisa and Garrett step out of the room. Lisa wipes her eyes, and I can tell she's been crying. Garrett places his arm around her shoulder and pulls her into a hug. She gives me a small wave behind his back, and they turn to leave.

I swallow down my nervousness, and then I leap up and ask, "Lisa, can I talk to you for a second before you go? It won't take a minute."

Garrett glances between us waiting to see what she says. She nods and places a hand on his arm.

"I'll be right there, just go on to the elevator."

We watch as he strides away.

"I have a million things to say to you, Lisa, but I don't want to take up too much of your time, so I'll make this short."

Her eyes watch me warily.

"I'm sorry for everything; for my relationship with Matt, for showing up on your doorstep, and for asking for money. I've never been sorrier in my life for anything. I'd say I'd take it back if I could, but to be quite honest I'd never give up Mariah. She's the best part of me. If I could, I would take away the hurt I caused you and what I've taken from you."

I point to the room where Judy is resting and inform her, "They all talk about you so much, I feel like I know you, and I'm not sure there is a better person out there.

"You shared Matt's estate with Mariah and got us in touch with his family. My daughter wouldn't have a family at all if it weren't for that. Thank God you helped again with money when I needed it the most. I was seeing Mariah so little I felt like she didn't know I was her mom before you upped the monthly allotment. You've given me time with my daughter I can never get back once it's gone. I know those things weren't easy for you, but they made a world of difference to me. I've wanted to send a letter to you a hundred times in the months since I've been here, but knew it wouldn't be appropriate. I just couldn't let you walk away today without saying thank you for saving our lives."

Tears are sliding down my face as I speak, and I try to wipe them away.

Her eyes are shiny, too, and she gives me a small smile. "I thought I would die when you showed up at my house. I had no idea anything was going on. If it weren't for you, I'd still be mourning a man who doesn't deserve it. Instead, I'm pregnant and getting married to a man who cherishes me and is excited for our baby. Judy told me you're seeing Johnny." She glances down at her feet and back up to me. "He's a great guy, and he will take care of you two. I know it's not easy trusting someone after Matt, but trust Johnny and be good to him.

"As for the estate, Mariah deserves it. I think Matt would have done the right thing eventually with her, but since he's not here to do that, I did it for him. Your daughter deserves your time and attention. The whole family told me what a good person you are, what a hard worker you are, and what a good mother you are, even Tara. All I ask is that you share yourself and your daughter with them. They love you both. Be happy, Jill. You deserve it, too."

"I met Garrett. He's really nice. He told me you're due in June. Congratulations. I hope you'll be happy."

"I already am."

"The rest of the Brownings are going to want to see you and meet your fiancé. If you call Steve or Johnny now, they are all together hanging out, I think. Well, minus Mary, she has my little girl so I can be here. Please stay in touch with them. It may be a little awkward for us, but it means so much to them."

"I will."

"Goodbye, Lisa."

"Goodbye, Jill."

I swipe at the remnants of tears on my face and tiptoe back into the hospital room hoping not to disturb Judy. I plop down in the chair and exhale thinking about the conversation I just had.

It's about that time when Judy says, "Well, that was awkward."

I bust up laughing. "Yeah, you can say that again, but it was okay, too. I was able to thank her for everything. She didn't know it, but she saved my life by having you call me. I've never been more thankful for anything."

Judy reaches her hand out to me and says, "Me

either. She's a good person, and so are you. I love you, Jill. Not just because of Mariah, but because of who you are. You've made Johnny so happy. I thought he'd never find anyone. I'm glad it's you. You belong with us."

"Thank you. I love you, too; all of you. I'll do my best to make Johnny happy. He's a good man, and I love him."

"I know, dear. It's written all over your face and has been since almost the first moment you saw each other. I've never seen anything like it. I felt it with John Sr. but I'd never seen it before with anyone else. I'm happy I was there to see the beginning of it."

We hold hands in silence after that, until hers goes limp with sleep. I tuck it under the covers and reflect on everything that's happened today.

****

Johnny

I need to call Jill and check on her, but her cell doesn't get good reception in the hospital. Who am I kidding? That piece of shit doesn't get good reception anywhere. She doesn't even get texts. Lisa and Garrett just left Dad's house, and I'm worried about how that encounter went for her. I heard Lisa's version, and it sounded all right, but who knows what's been going through Jill's head. It was great to see Lisa and meet her new man. He's a good guy from what I can tell, and he takes good care of her.

She floored me right before she left when she hugged me and said, "Take good care of your girls. I think they were always meant to be yours, and this was the only way for you to get them. You deserve each other. You're a good man. You always have been, and I think she's a good woman. Treat her like that always. Don't ever take for granted what a gift they are. I love you, Johnny."

Before I could respond, she strode down the walkway to where Garrett was holding the car door open for her, wiggled her fingers at all of us, and was gone.

I leave my family and go to the Verizon store. I buy a new iPhone, pay for a plan for a year, and put it in her name. Then I drive to the hospital and go to Mom's room. As I enter, I notice that Mom is talking with Jill. When Jill sees me, her face splits into a huge grin. I can't help but return it. She jumps up and runs for me. That's my kind of hello.

"You okay?" I whisper in her ear.

"Yeah, I'm good. I've had some quality time with your mom, and I saw Lisa."

I search her eyes as I ask, "How did that go?"

She seems far more relaxed than she ever has been when she answers. "It was actually good. I was able to thank her for everything and apologize. I needed to do both of those things and thought I'd never get the chance. She was really sweet and seemed happy. Did she call you?"

"Yes, we saw her for a couple of hours. It was nice. It's also why I showed up here. I couldn't get you on that ancient piece of crap phone to check on you, so I bought you a new one. No arguing. Service is paid in full for a year. I'll show you how to use it, but you have to dump the other one. How can I sext you when you don't get texts?"

She slaps my chest playfully as her cheeks burn red with embarrassment. "Johnny! Your mother is in the room."

Mom pipes up from behind her, "Oh, honey, please. If he's anything like his father, you'll get at least ten of those sext things a day."

Jill doubles over laughing as I groan, "Moooom. That's something I never want to know about you two."

Chapter Nine

Jill
Two Months later

Life has been good with Johnny. We stay at his place most of the time, but there are some nights we stay at mine. I'm still working downtown, so my hours are long. Johnny offered me a job as a receptionist/office manager at his auto shop last week. The salary is better than what I've been making, benefits are good, and I won't have to drive downtown every day. He'll have to train me himself since the girl who held the position already quit and moved to Arizona with her boyfriend.

It doesn't sound like a difficult job, and he assures me that I'm more than capable of doing it, but I'm afraid he'll get sick of me if we are with each other too much. He's giving me another week to decide, and I'm taking my time giving the answer. I just don't know if that's the best thing for us, and *us* is way more important to me than a better job.

What if I start that job and Johnny realizes I'm not smart enough to do it, or I screw something major up? That could cause serious problems and I don't know if I'm confident enough with my abilities to risk what I have with him personally for the opportunity.

As I continue to roll these thoughts over in my mind, I pull into the driveway of his little ranch style house to find a small, white Ford Focus parked in his spot. I have no idea whose car it is, so I scan the front of the house and find Mindy sitting in the rocker on the front porch.

Something about her is different, but I can't quite put my finger on it. What is she doing here? As far as I know, Johnny hasn't seen her since before we hooked up. I remove Mariah from her car seat and set her on my hip. I lift her diaper bag over my shoulder and walk in her direction. The sun is setting and the air is cooling down, so I tug Mariah's sweater tighter across her chest and climb the stairs.

"Hi, Mindy. What are you doing here?"

"I want to see Johnny, and he won't return my calls."

He didn't tell me she's been calling him. Why wouldn't he tell me she's been calling?

"I don't know when he'll be home. He's been taking care of his mom and has been getting home at different times every night"

"Can you call him? I really need to see him."

Alarm bells go off in my brain and a sliver of unease rolls over me. About that time, Cici pulls into the driveway next door and climbs out of her car. She takes in the situation with assessing eyes, waves, and hollers, "Hey Jill! I'll be over in about five minutes, I just need to change."

I've spent enough time with her now to understand that she knows we don't have plans, but realizes I need a buffer for Mindy.

I yell back, "Okay, see you in a few."

I turn to Mindy and say, "I'll have Johnny call you when he gets home."

I'm starting to lose my hold on the squirming baby in my hands, so I put my key in the door and push my way in. Her eyes narrow on me and her hands shift to her hips.

"You live here now?" It's more of an accusation than a question.

"No, just visiting." I try for nonchalance. Something isn't right, and it's got the hair on the back of my neck standing on end.

"You fucking Johnny?" She blurts out the crass question as she narrows her eyes on me. It's then that I notice the circles under her eyes and realize what's different is she's slightly unkempt. Which is strange since the others times I'd seen her she was practically perfect. I thought she was one of those women that never left the house in less than full makeup and hair.

"That's not your business. I think it's time for you to leave. I'll tell him you were here."

As I step farther into the doorway, she tries to follow so I twist at the waist and set Mariah down on her feet. Then before she can push in, I pull the door against my side blocking her entrance, the whole time I'm praying that Cici will show up quickly.

Her face turns lobster red, and her eyes narrow further.

"Were you fucking him when I was with him? I knew there was a reason he wouldn't fuck me. Are you the reason he broke things off? We were doing well. I shouldn't be surprised. I heard you were a home wrecker; guess that applies to boyfriends, too. You'll be sorry; nobody takes what's mine." She snarls at me, spins on her heel, and stomps off toward her car. Cici steps onto the porch about the time that Mindy is pulling away.

"What was that about, Jill?"

"She showed up here, because she didn't get the memo that things are over. Then she accused me of sleeping with Johnny while they were together and called me a home wrecker." I sigh, tired from the drama and usher Cici into the house.

She crouches down on the floor, sweeps a giggling Mariah up into her arms, and pops a loud kiss on her cheek. "Hey, squirt!"

Mariah squirms to get free, so Cici puts her down and plants her butt into the corner of Johnny's couch. I leave the room to change into more comfortable clothes and grab two beers as I return. Cici takes a long drink of hers before she asks, "Do you think Mindy could turn out to be a problem for you or Johnny?"

"I have no idea. She's not right in the head, that's for sure. I'm not sure what she's capable of besides just being pushy. I'll talk to Johnny about it tonight."

"In my line of work, I've seen my fair share of crazies, so I can spot them at a hundred yards. She certainly has my internal alarm going off. Call the cops if she shows up again. You can always call Denton or me, too. Don't take any chances."

Cici stays with me until Johnny arrives, which is partially to do with the strange Mindy visit and partially our new thing, I think. I've grown to really like Cici and the time we hang out. She's genuine, spunky, and just plain cool as hell.

Since I've been staying here more, if she sees my car in the driveway, she comes over when she gets home from work just to shoot the shit for a little bit. It's nice. Between her, Mary, and Valerie from my old job,

I've decided that I don't ever want to go without girlfriends again. Life is better with them in it.

When Johnny walks through the door, it doesn't take long for him to figure out this is not our ordinary girly-giggle fest as he calls them. Most of the time, she's gone by the time he arrives. Cici excuses herself, and I wait to lock the door behind her before I tell him about my afternoon.

"Why didn't you tell me Mindy's been calling you?"

I'm a little irritated, and I'm certain he can tell that by the hands-on-my-hips, head tilted, scowl I'm giving him.

"Because I didn't care that she was calling, and I wasn't answering. How do you know that?"

"It wasn't because I was snooping, but it does make me wonder what else you're not telling me. Mindy was waiting on the porch today when I got here. She was a little hostile and pretty insistent that she needs to talk to you. I think you need to call her. She got really upset and asked if I was living with you and fucking you. Then she called me a home wrecker and said it must apply to boyfriends, too. It was a lovely visit." The sarcasm is thick in my voice.

Johnny leans over, picks up Mariah, kisses her cheek, and she giggles as she turns to smear a slobbery kiss on him.

"How did you answer her?"

"I told her I was just visiting, and it wasn't any of her business if I was fucking you or not. I would have said yes, just to match her bitch attitude if my eleven-month-old daughter wasn't toddling around on the floor in your living room. I don't trust Mindy, and I got a bad feeling while she was here."

"What does all of that have to do with Cici?"

"She pulled in the driveway as Mindy was grilling me and came over as a buffer once she got changed. I think she stuck around because she was a little nervous Mindy might come back. I'm not sure Mindy's stable. How long ago did you break up?"

"About three months ago, I think. Are you okay?" The concern is evident in his voice.

"Yeah, it just made me nervous with Mariah here. Call her and get it over with so she'll stay away, please."

"Okay, I will. I'll call once we get the baby down for the night. I want you present to hear whatever she's going to say."

"You don't have to, but if it makes you feel better, that's okay with me."

About an hour later, Johnny is hanging up the phone after a ten-minute heated discussion with Mindy. He had her on speakerphone so I could hear every single word. Apparently, she's been calling since he ended it months ago. She's also been coming by the house, but it must have been on nights that we were at my place. I'm thinking she's moved past unstable to flat out crazy, and that worries me.

Things have been going so well for me these last few months that I've been waiting for something bad to happen. I've never been this happy in my life, and I don't trust it. I realize this is a bad attitude to have, but I can't seem to help it.

Before we can talk about it anymore, Johnny scoops me up into his arms and carries me to his room. My clothes are removed one piece at a time and his roughened fingers trail lightly along the newly exposed skin. He peels off each piece, bringing up goose bumps in their wake. Once he lays me on the bed, he kisses his way from my feet to my mouth, stopping briefly to tease the delicate folds of my sex with his lips and tongue. His fingers graze the skin around my taut nipple, but refuse any direct stimulation. It drives me mad with want for him, and he knows it. Anticipation is an art form to this man. Just as I'm about to explode from the tension he's drawn tight in my body, he rolls to his back taking me with him.

"Ride me, baby. I need to watch you work for it. I want to see your perfect tits bounce and those sexy hips roll."

His words stoke the fire as I take him inside me, sinking down on him. I close my eyes and throw my head back as I slowly roll my hips like he asked. I'm drawing out the growing sensation for both of us.

Lightning flashes outside, and the thunder cracks somewhere close by, but I don't break my stride. Every time I grind down a noise escapes his throat that helps to build me higher. His hands caress my stomach, across my breasts and then up into the back of my hair as he jackknifes up into a sitting position. Our lips are touching, but we aren't kissing. We are exchanging breaths, our eyes locked on each other as something more than an orgasm builds between us. He grips my hair in his fist and pulls back to expose my neck.

The cacophony of rain pelting the roof and windows now adds a new sound to our lovemaking. Johnny licks my neck and sucks hard enough that I know it'll leave a mark. "Johnny…" I breathe but can't finish the thought.

"You're mine. I don't care who asks. The answer is always I'm yours and you're mine. Understand? I need to know that we're it for each other, and I want to know you have no problem saying it. Tell me, baby. Who do you belong to?"

I'm moving faster now. Turned on by his talk of possession and claiming. My body is hanging on at the point of detonation. One little shift of his hips, one pinch of my nipple, or even one tug of my hair and I'll spiral into the abyss. A whimper of need escapes me. Coherent thoughts are gone and my body is ready.

"Tell me, Jillian. Tell me you're mine. Tell me I'm yours. I need to hear you say it." His hand slides between us, and he's a millimeter away from touching my clit. I need him to take care of me; I *need* him to touch me. Right. Now.

"Jill." He says through clenched teeth.

His eyes burn like emeralds on fire.

"I love you, Johnny. You're mine, and I'm yours, and I'll tell everyone." The words rush out, breathy and ragged.

His mouth crashes to mine as his pointer finger makes contact, stroking me with only a couple of rough strokes, and I erupt like a volcano around him. He flips me to my back and plows into me with more force than he ever has, extending my climax until he comes so hard I swear I feel it in my chest.

His muscles relax, allowing his tattoos to smooth out and he rests on top of me, putting just enough weight on me to feel safe, but not enough to crush me. I run my hands over his sweaty body and sniff the musky smell of sweat on his neck before I lick and suck making sure to leave a mark to match the one he gave me.

I grip his hair and pull his head up making eye contact with him.

"I love you, Johnny. Don't ever doubt that. I'll tell everyone if you want me to. I just want you to be happy."

"I am happier than I've ever been in my life with you. Tell me again."

"I love you." I tell him against his lips, finding it hard not to smile as I say it.

The rain patters on the roof as we lie entwined in each other's arms.

"You've heard me tell Mindy to stay away from you. If she shows up anywhere near you, please call the cops. I may have to get a restraining order against her to keep her away. I think she might be a little messed up in the head. If she knocks on our door, don't answer it. I'm serious; something isn't right with her."

"I kind of figured that out already, but I promise not to answer the door for her."

"Have you thought any more about the job?"

"What if I screw up and it doesn't work out? It'll be awkward as hell for you to fire me and then I have to start over looking for another job. I know it's a great opportunity, but I'm afraid it will ruin us."

"Honey, it's not rocket science. You're more than capable of doing this job. In fact, you'll probably do it better than Janelle did. She never really cared about the business or me. You love me, so I know you'll take care of things. Come on, baby, just try it. If you hate it, I won't be upset if you want to leave. I promise to be honest if it isn't working for me, too. Okay?"

The lightning flashes bright enough outside the

window that I can see the expression on his face, and it melts me.

"Yes, baby. I'll come work for you. Let me put in my notice tomorrow. I'll give two weeks. You can start training me on the weekend if you want."

"You really will?"

"Yes."

His smile is so bright it can be seen through the darkness. His excitement is palpable, literally growing between us. Before I can utter another word, he flips me onto my stomach, pulls me up to my knees by the hips, and plows into me full force. How did he recover that quickly? I didn't even realize that was a possibility. My body shakes with his forceful rhythm as he grips harder on my hips to steady me. My screams echo off the walls and for a brief moment I wonder if I'll wake the baby before I even come.

****

Three weeks later, I'm buried in paperwork at Johnny's office. Janelle, the woman who worked here before me, had not been filing invoices, or making deposits, or doing much of anything. I can't figure out what she was doing all day, but it's now my job to get all of this straightened out. Johnny worked with me every day the first week and plans to come back once I get to a point where I need more help. He's taken his mom to a doctor's appointment this afternoon. His dad just went back to work this week, and they've worked it out for Johnny to be with her for all the necessities for now.

It's been great having more time with Mariah in the morning and more time with both her and Johnny at night. What a difference just a few hours has made in our lives. This morning at breakfast, Johnny asked us to move in with him. When I stared at him, horrified, I think his feelings were hurt a little. He dropped the subject and slipped into silent mode before he left for his mom's. I'm praying he's not still upset with me. I didn't mean for him to see that expression or misinterpret it. I just don't know if me moving in all the way, right after we've started working together, is such a good idea. I didn't get a chance to explain, because he took off so quick.

He sent me a text around eight o'clock that said he was going to spend time with his brother before he came home. By eleven, dog-tired I fall asleep on the couch waiting for him.

Click, bang, click.

"Shit." These are the sounds that rouse me from my slumber.

I lift my head peering over the back of the couch to see Johnny stumble into the house. The door is left standing wide open, and he's banging from wall to wall like a pinball in a machine on his way to the bedroom before I can even say anything. I'm sure he saw me there, but he just ignored me and banged his way down the hall.

I shut and lock the front door before I follow him into the bedroom.

"Johnny?"

He won't look at me, and it's obvious by his clumsy movements he's drunk.

"Johnny, why are you ignoring me?"

He finally gets his shirt and shoes off and crashes onto the mattress on his back with one arm shielding his eyes and the other one limp at his side. Socks still cover his feet and his jeans are unbuttoned, but still zipped.

"Johnny, talk to me, honey. What's going on?"

"You won't talk to me, so I don't have to talk to you," he slurs.

"That's not true, Johnny. You didn't give me a chance to respond this morning."

"Your face said what you couldn't." The smell of whiskey floods my nose while he speaks. It's so strong I'm wondering if he swam in it instead of drinking it.

"That's not true, honey. We can talk in the morning when you're sober. Let me help you get your jeans off." He grunts and lays there like a giant, heavy, limp noodle. I tug and jerk to get his jeans off, but he's already dead weight. I'm sweating and panting from exertion by the time I get them off. I leave his boxers on and remove his socks. Then I work the covers out from under him and pull them up over both of us. I scoot over to cuddle up to him, and that's when I get a whiff of it.

Perfume.

A brand I've never in my life worn, and it's heavy on his neck.

"What the hell?" I yell, but he doesn't flutter an eyelash.

My blood is boiling I'm so pissed. Has he been with someone else? Did he sleep with her? Oh my god, I can't believe this is happening, and I can't even ask him about it. I throw the covers off and storm out of the room with my phone in hand. I lay down in the spare bedroom, mad as hell at him. How could he do this to me? Knowing what I went through with Matt and what kind of trust issues I have. One wrong facial expression and he's off with some other woman? He didn't even give us a chance to fight about it this morning. Instead of coming home to talk about it, he took comfort in another woman. It's a good thing I figured this out before I moved in here. The problem I realize is that I work for him now. I can't even go to work to get away from him. I knew taking that job was a bad idea. I can't freaking believe it. My heart hammers in my chest as I clench the sheets in my fists. I'm so damn angry and can't do anything about it.

I'm not sure if I ever really fall asleep, or if I just doze off for a few minutes. My alarm is making a racket, and I am exhausted. I've also passed the point of pissed off right on to hurt.

I dress and feed Mariah faster than normal and drop her off early at daycare. I don't want to be at the house when he wakes up, so I haul ass to work and plow through stacks of paperwork. The one good thing about getting mad is it lights a fire under my ass, and I get twice as much done in half the time.

Around noon, Johnny comes dragging in. I won't look at him, and I won't speak to him. I keep working. A slow burn seated right in my chest has morphed into an inferno of epic proportions. I'm either going to freak out or throw up. I don't want to do either here at work, so I clock out and leave to go find lunch away from the office. I come back forty-five minutes later and clock back in. Johnny is sitting at my desk just watching me move around the room.

"Are you ever going to talk to me, Jill?"

"I don't think that's a good idea here, Johnny."

"Why?"

"Because I'm on the clock, and I have to earn a paycheck, not argue with the boss."

"I'll clock you out then," he states in a matter-of-fact tone.

"Don't you dare. You know I need the paycheck, Johnny."

"Why are you so mad? I know I drank too much last night, but I didn't know it would be a problem for you."

My eyes bug out of my head like a Ren and Stimpy cartoon. My mouth gapes unattractively. "Coming home drunk is not the issue, Johnny, and you know it. Did you think I wouldn't find out? Did you think I wouldn't care?" My voice is shrill as I shake from head to toe so flipping mad I can't stand it.

"What are you talking about, Jill?"

"I'm talking about the woman's perfume that you stunk of last night. It was all over your face, neck, and chest. I'm not okay with you running to some other woman. After all I've been through, I can't believe you'd go there. How fucking cruel can you be?" I'm shouting at him.

I rush out of the room to the bathroom and lock the door. I'm sure the whole shop heard my melt down. All of that emotion was sitting just under the surface waiting for a break-out moment, allowing all of my insecurities to come screaming back to life.

About ten minutes go by, and I'm finally starting to calm down when I hear a *tap, tap, tap* on the door.

"Open the door, Jilli. We have to talk, now."

I don't reply I just let the tears slide down my face. The cold tile of the floor under my butt and the wall at my back have me shivering, but I don't want to move. I don't want to face him or this situation. I've trusted him from the beginning, and he stomped on that.

Tap, tap, tap, louder this time.

"Open up, Jilli. We need to talk this out. It's not what you think, and I can prove it."

Stubborn is the reigning emotion of the moment, so I refuse to move. I hear retreating footsteps and a minute later, I hear the same heavy footsteps returning. Keys jingle on the other side of the door right before it whooshes open, and he holds up a key to show me how he got in. Then he sits next to me on the floor with his heels close to his butt, arms stretched out casually over his bent knees.

"It's Mary's perfume. I didn't see anyone else last night. Steve needed help dragging me to the cab and apparently, I keep rolling into her since she's so much smaller than he is. You can call and ask her. You didn't notice my truck missing this morning? I'm surprised she hasn't called to tell you all about it already, to be quite honest. I understand why you'd jump to that conclusion, but I swear I'd never cheat on you. I have no interest in anyone else. I was just hurt and upset all day yesterday, and I didn't want to hear you tell me that you aren't serious enough about me to move in.

"We spend every night together. We haven't slept apart since we got together that first night. I couldn't understand why you'd look like I just kicked your puppy when I only wanted to make sharing a bed together official.

"I love you, Jillian, but I feel like I have to fight you every step of the way. I just want you to look at me and say 'I love you, I belong to you, and there's nowhere else I'd rather be.' I now realize that's not going to happen, and it hurts."

"That's not true. I never said it wasn't going to

happen. I didn't say anything. You didn't even give me a chance to process it. Haven't you figured out by now that I need time to think everything through? I can't make decisions on the fly, especially, big ones that should be thought out."

My fingers pick at an invisible thread on my slacks for a few seconds before I look up at him sheepishly through my lashes and ask, "Was that really Mary's perfume?"

"Yes. I didn't realize I'd have it all over me, but that was the only woman I was with last night. I drank at Steve's house. I never went to a bar, never left their house except to come home in the cab. The cab driver wasn't even a woman; it was a three-hundred-pound man with a walrus mustache and a beret.

"I told you that you were mine and I'm yours and I meant that. No matter how mad or hurt I am, I won't work it out with another woman under me. It just takes me time to calm down."

"I want to move in with you. I want to marry you. I want to have your babies, if you want them, but I'm scared. I'm fearful that if we move too fast it will blow up in my face. Everything I've ever wanted is right in front of me, and I'm worried that if I rush in to it I'll find that it was only a mirage."

"What we have is no mirage. It's the real deal. We're the lucky ones. We found who we want, and we don't have to wait if we don't want to. If you need to keep waiting, then we will, but we spend every night together as it is. We work together, and you're at my place most of the time. Wouldn't it be nice if it were *our* place? If we didn't have to go back and forth to get clothes or other stuff? It would also eliminate rent for you. Think about it. I won't push you anymore. Just know that you're the one I want, and I want you with me, always."

He stands up and hoists me from the floor into his arms. I nuzzle his chest and take a deep breath. The smell of his body soap and clean shirt relax me. I lift my chin and offer my lips. His mouth covers mine in a slow sensual kiss that leaves me weak in the knees.

"I love you, Jill. Don't let the ghosts in your head tell you any different."

"I'm sorry I flipped out. The thought of any woman close enough to you to leave her scent all over your clothing makes me crazy with jealousy. I love you, too. I'll move in with you. I know I was being stupid, and I would have come to that conclusion if you'd given me a little bit of time. Just be patient with me. I'm trying to wipe away all the grime of my past, but it takes time."

****

We move my stuff in over the weekend, and I'm able to get out of my lease without an issue. Thank goodness there is now a waiting list for this complex, so I didn't have to pay to break the lease.

Tuesday afternoon, I notice an unfamiliar blue car follow me to the bank as I make the drop for the shop. It follows me back to the shop and drives slowly past as I get out of the car to walk inside. The windows are tinted too dark to see who is driving, but it gives me the willies, big time. On Wednesday, the same car follows me to the daycare and home afterward. I'm so scared that I call Cici and have her and Denton meet me in the driveway.

Johnny is still helping his parents out a lot and

wasn't there to greet me when I got home and isn't riding with me to the shop every day. I hadn't told him about Tuesday because I thought I was being paranoid, but Denton says I have to tell him today. Denton also gave me his cell number and said if I can't get a hold of Johnny or Cici, that I should call him.

They wait with me until he gets home around eight o'clock and sit with me while I tell him the story. Denton tells him that he gave me his number and why. Johnny is rightfully concerned and figures it's Mindy, but since I couldn't see her, I can't prove it. Johnny already tried to file a complaint with the police last week, but they said unless we had proof, they couldn't do anything about it.

****

Thursday is peaceful. There is no one following me, and I am able to finish getting the office cleaned up all the way. Files are in the cabinet alphabetized, invoices are cleared or mailed, all payments are logged into the system, and all drops have been made to the bank. I'm feeling pretty proud of myself.

Chapter Ten

Jill

Monday morning starts like any other week with too much going on. Several cars had come in over the weekend, so Johnny is in the shop with the guys all morning, and I'm working on payroll. Around eleven-thirty, Johnny strolls into the office and asks if I can pick up lunch for everyone, so I leave. I return about forty-five minutes later with my purse over my shoulder and my arms full of bags and boxes of food. I take everything to the break room and start setting things down when I hear someone yelling outside of the office. I hustle back out there and find Mindy, looking crazy and out of control, screaming at Eduardo, Johnny's shop manager. I step into full view and ask, "What's going on?"

Her eyes snap to mine, and the look of hate she shoots my way should melt me in my shoes. She pushes past Eduardo to come after me, but he snags her by both elbows and pulls her flush against him with a grunt. That sets her off further.

"Why are you keeping him from me? You afraid if he sees me he'll want me back?"

Her screeching is so loud as she struggles to get out of his grip that I'm surprised the whole shop hasn't come in to see what's going on.

"I'm not keeping anything from you, Mindy. It's

his choice who he sees. He's a grown man."

I looked past her to Eduardo and ask, "Where's Johnny?"

"I told him to stay out there. I don't want him to get arrested because of her. He's supposed to be calling the cops since she won't leave."

Why won't she go away? I pop my hip out and place my hands on my hips. "Why are you here? He's told you he's not interested. He's told you not to call or come around. Do you want to get arrested?"

"He won't call the cops on me. I know he won't. He wants me back, he just doesn't know how to get rid of you, but I can handle that for him." She snarls.

Before I can say another word, two uniformed officers walk through the door.

"What the fuck?" she yells.

The first cop looks at Eduardo and says, "We got a call about a problem, I'm guessing this is it?"

He nods but can't speak as he continues to try and hold her.

"Miss, you have to calm down. This is a place of business. I'm going to ask the gentleman to let you go, but if you don't settle down, I will cuff you."

Eduardo releases her and steps in front of me as if he's protecting me.

"I just want to see Johnny! They're keeping him from me!" Her hands are laced in her ratty hair, and she's pulling it out of sheer frustration.

Officer number two speaks up this time, "Miss, John Browning called the station and complained that you've been asked to stay away before and when you showed up today, you were asked to leave but refused. He does not want to see you. If you don't walk yourself out of here, I'll have you arrested for trespassing. This is your final warning."

She lets out a wild banshee scream and storms out of the room. As the door closes behind her, my head falls to Eduardo's shoulder. Her level of crazy is draining.

Officer number two followed Mindy out of the building when she left, and officer number one says to me, "I think you should file a report in case this happens again. She doesn't seem very stable. We will make sure she leaves the premises now and will increase patrol cars in the area for the next few days. That's about all we can do for now, though."

I release a tired sigh. "Thank you for coming. I appreciate it. I'll talk to Johnny, and we will come in to file a report."

"I'd like to speak with Mr. Browning before I leave if that's possible."

"Sure, I'll go find him."

I click on my heels out across the cement floor of the shop in search of Johnny. I see the edge of one tattooed elbow peeking out from under the hood of a Toyota sedan so I call his name.

His head appears, and his expression changes.

"What are you doing here? I thought you'd gone to get food. Please tell me Mindy was gone when you got here."

"No, I'm afraid not. The police are here now. They want to speak to you. Mindy left, and the other officer followed her to make sure she left the property."

"I'm sorry, baby. I didn't think you'd be back during all of that. Are you okay?"

He wipes his hands on a half-greasy towel and

follows me inside.

"I'm fine. She's bat-shit-crazy, but I'm okay. We owe Eduardo. He looked like an alligator wrestler the way he had to hold onto her."

Johnny spends the next fifteen minutes talking to the police and then all three of us drive to the police station to file a report. I have a bad feeling we haven't seen the last of her.

****

The rest of the week passes without incident, but I've kept my guard up. I just have an awful feeling she's going to resurface at the most inopportune moment.

At two-thirty on Friday afternoon, Johnny is out of the office taking Judy to an appointment when I get a text from him explaining that Mary and Steve are picking up the baby from daycare and keeping her tonight, because he has a special night planned for us.

Butterflies swarm in my stomach at the thought of what that might mean. He instructs me to leave work a half an hour early to get ready and wear the dress he left out on the bed. I smile a mile wide and shut down my computer so I can head home.

Never having someone do something like this for me before has me giddy with excitement. I rush home not paying attention to anything around me. I jam my key in the door and twist. It pops right open, and I push through. I dump my purse on the couch and hurry back to the bedroom to see what dress he's chosen.

My feet stop abruptly as my mind tries to process the scene in front of me. The dress Johnny picked is laid across the bed, and Mindy is sitting right next to it with one leg crossed over the other. She's wearing a sinister grin and holding a piece of paper in her hand. By the look of her, I'm not sure when she showered last. Her hair is greasy and unkempt, way worse than when we saw her Monday. Her clothes are sloppy and have probably been on her body for over a week. She's not wearing any makeup, and the look in her eyes tells me she passed crazy a long time ago. Crap.

"What are you doing here, Mindy?" I clear my throat trying to push the shaky quality out of it.

"I decided it's time to come take back what's mine. By the look of this note and the dress he's left out, I have my work cut out for me. It's good that I'm up for the task."

"Johnny will be here any time now. How about if we wait in the living room for him, and you guys can talk."

"Nope, I'm done talking. You stole him right out from under me, and I plan to rectify that. Calling the cops the other day only pissed me off more."

Fear cements my feet to the floor as my brain screams *run!* Before I can get more than two steps away, she's on me, the weight of her body smacking me into the wall in the hallway. Clutching my hair, she slams my head into the wall repeatedly until my vision is hazy and my muscles go limp.

Panic fires up my fight-or-flight response even in the fog that my brain is swimming in, and I squirm to get away from her. When that doesn't work, I kick out and buck my body. Her clawed fingers dig into my scalp, and streaks of pain shoot through me. Then her fist connects with my jaw, and the world goes black.

Unsure of how much time has gone by, a throbbing pain in my head and a burning on my wrists cuts through the cloudy feeling as I wake up disoriented. The severity of my situation comes back to me when I realize I'm in an extremely uncomfortable position.

Crazy Mindy is in our house. She's tied my hands and feet together too tightly in front of me, and the rope is cutting into my skin. She left me on the living room floor and hasn't covered my mouth, so I try to scream. The only noise that comes out is a squeak. Dread floods my system, and I worry that she's done something to my voice. My throat burns and my muscles ache with cramping from the awkward position she has me tied up in. I continue to squeak hoping that a scream will come out if I keep trying.

I lift my head twisting it around like an owl scanning for a threat, and I don't see her anywhere, so I do a painful, awkward drag-scoot out of the hallway toward the door. My elbows bang on the hardwood floor and send daggers of pain through my arms to my shoulders. My ribs are screaming with each movement, and I'm certain she's landed a few kicks in them while I was out. I make it to the doorway of the house and fight to stand or crouch. I think that's as much as the slack in the rope will let me do. If I can't get up, I'll never get the door open.

I lean my back against the door and thrust with my legs, heaving my body into motion. It takes several tries, but I finally get upright. My head swims with the change in position, and my vision blurs for a moment. I feel around grasping the handle with my chin. My arms won't stretch up that far to work the door handle. I can't get a good grip on it to turn no matter how hard I squeeze my chin to my chest. I keep trying, but it's no use.

My already rapid breathing is going crazy, and I'm in danger of passing out. It's then she comes out of my room wearing the dress that Johnny left on the bed for me. It's ill-fitting since we aren't the same size. Her breasts are popping out of the top, and possibly it will split along the seams it's pulled so tight through the hips. She's run a brush through her hair, but she's still greasy looking. She's also plastered on heavy makeup, and scary is the proper word for the look in her eyes.

I panic and swivel my body the best I can. I smash my head into the glass panel by the doorknob and start screaming. I'm so excited sound is finally coming from my throat that I forget to be scared for a second. Blood gushes from my head, and the tangy scent of copper fills my nose and mouth, but I try to scream around it. Again, the weird squeaky sound is back and then it morphs into a full shriek, and I keep going until *whoosh*, the breath is knocked out of me. Something solid and hard connects with my back smashing me into the door before I sink to the floor to writhe in pain.

Mindy rushes from the room and comes back screaming while waving a gun around, "Don't fucking move, you home-wrecking bitch! He's mine, and you won't ruin our night. Get your ass back in here."

She growls before she grabs my feet and drags me back away from the door. My breath has returned, but my whole body is quaking with fear. I know if I give in, I'll never walk out of here alive. I start screaming again, clawing onto anything I can grab with limited mobility as she pulls me away. I manage to throw her against the nearest wall with the power of a double leg thrust and scoot awkwardly backward with my feet still tied together. I use my elbows and the coffee table to climb up and hop toward the door. I'm almost there when I'm knocked clean off my feet as the sound of a gunshot bounces through the room. Searing pain burns into my back, through my chest, and I feel myself falling, and the world goes black.

Chapter Eleven

Johnny

I've been excited all day. I don't think anyone has done anything like this for Jill before. I love seeing the look on her face when something good happens and I know I'll be seeing that look a lot tonight as I have a big night planned for us.

Oddly, as I'm turning into my driveway I see Denton and Cici running full speed from their house to mine. Both have guns in their hands, up and in front of them like actors in a cop show. Dread fills my gut and I slam the truck into park and jump out rounding the vehicle at a dead sprint.

"What the fuck?" I yell.

Denton pauses. Cici keeps running.

"We heard screaming and were already coming out the door when a gunshot sounded. Call 911!" He yells over to me.

Cici is on the porch peering sideways through my front door. I dial 911 as I hustle toward her, and before I can hit send on my phone, Cici is firing through the glass paned portion of my door. Two shots total, I think. My mind is reeling, and all logical thought is gone in an instant. I drop my phone and run. I hear an odd noise and a thump. I don't stop. I grab the knob only to realize it's still locked. "Shit!" I shout. Most of the door panes are busted, and jagged glass surrounds them. My keys are still in the car, and I can see two women lying on the floor motionless.

"Call 911!" I scream. "Oh my God, call 911! Jill! Baby, I'm here. Oh fuck, oh fuck!"

I slice my hands on broken panels of jagged glass as I get the door open and rush through. It's like a scene out of a horror movie. The metallic smell of blood permeates the air, and Jill is face down on the floor. There's a trail of blood leading to her lifeless body like she's been dragged several feet from the door. Mindy is on her back wide-eyed and motionless. One shot got her in the neck leaving a bloody raw mess and the other in her chest. I register that she's wearing the dress I bought for Jill today, but I'm too freaked out to care.

I roll Jill over as gingerly as possible. The front of her shirt is sopping wet with blood, and I can't tell where all of it is coming from. Her face and hair are matted with it, and it's everywhere. My panic rises another notch when it becomes obvious she isn't breathing, and if she is, it's intermittent. I can hear Denton on the phone talking to the 911 operator. Cici has found a knife from the kitchen and is trying to cut the rope off Jill's hands and feet.

She's crying and chanting, "Come on, Jill. Hold on. Hold on. Hold on."

I'm not sure if chest compressions are a good idea with all the blood in that area, so I just do mouth to mouth. I hope I'm doing the right thing because I'm terrified, and all kinds of crazy things are rushing through my mind.

I hear the ambulance getting closer, and the next thing I know a guy in a uniform is pushing me out of the way and asking questions that Cici and I are both trying to answer. The police come through the door a minute later and start asking questions. I'm freaking out about Jill and trying to follow the gurney. Cici and Denton are doing their best to answer all of the cop's questions. I don't even think or ask permission, I just jump into the ambulance with the paramedics as we head for the hospital.

When we arrive, Jill is rushed through the doors into the bowels of the ER and a tall, gangly, middle-aged receptionist approaches me. "Sir, I have some paperwork for you to fill out. The nurses may have questions, too. Can I call someone to be with you?"

I blink repeatedly trying to understand what she's just said to me.

"Sir? Can I call someone for you?"

"Yeah, I need my brother. My cell phone is in my truck at home. I don't know the number."

A helpless feeling washes though me, and I drop into the nearest chair, I'm shaking as the adrenaline leaves my body.

"Sir, give me his name and an address, if you have it. I'll find him."

The shakes seem to be getting worse so I wrap my arms around my middle and say, "Steve Browning. Steve and Mary. They live on Maple Way in Batavia. I don't know the exact address."

"Okay, I'll find them. Does your wife have any allergies?"

"My girlfriend. Jillian Pierce. No, I don't think so."

"Does she have any other family?"

"No, just my family."

"Hold tight. I'll find your brother. You need to go wash up."

My eyes shift to my hands and arms, and I'm horrified to realize they are covered in Jill's blood where I tried to hold her. Tears spill from my eyes as it dawns on me that she probably won't make it out of here alive. I'm not even sure she was alive when she came in. I choke back a sob. If I start, I won't stop. I just need my brother and my dad. I can't go through this without them.

I stumble to the bathroom and do my best to wash off in the sink. Rivers of red-pink-tinged water swirl around in the sink, and I brace my hands on the sides to keep from dropping to the floor. Reality is flooding in, and I can't believe I'm here. I can't believe any of this has happened.

Somehow, I end up back in the waiting room and what seems like forever goes by before I see Steve rush in through the automatic doors followed closely by my dad, my sister, and Bobby. Tara waddle-runs around everyone to get to me and throws her arms around me, squishing my middle with her pregnant belly. She's crying hard, and I can't understand what she's saying. Bobby peels her off me and tries to calm her down. Steve and my dad surround me in a weird group hug. That is my undoing. I lose it as my body quakes with sobs. I'm certain I've never cried this hard before. I've never felt so helpless in my life.

"What's going on, Johnny?" Steve asks concerned.

"I don't know. They haven't told me anything yet."

"Denton called Dad from your phone and told him to get here ASAP. About the same time, I was getting a call from a woman named Vera here at the hospital telling me to come quickly. We didn't get any details. Are you okay?"

"No. I'm not okay. Mindy broke into the house before I got home and beat Jill pretty badly and then shot her. She wasn't breathing when I found her. Cici killed Mindy. Shot her right in the throat and the chest. I don't know how Mindy got into the house. I'm so glad Mariah wasn't with her. Oh God, what if Jill's dead? Oh God. I can't do this."

My father's stern voice breaks through the hysteria, "Son, you need to settle down. Jill will be okay. We're here for you, and we're going to help you get through this, but you have to hold it together."

His strong hands clench my shoulders, and he shakes me a little trying to make his point. I fall apart again. My brother puts his arms around me and hugs me like he did when we were little and we found out our grandpa had died. Normally this kind of emotion would embarrass me, but I don't give a shit. The only thing I care about is dying or dead somewhere in this hospital. After I calm down, Steve coaxes me outside for a little bit of fresh air with the promise from my dad that they will grab me if they hear anything at all.

Hours later, we're alternating between sitting and pacing. Tara refuses to leave even after we all begged her to go home and rest. I feel like a zombie—lifeless and cold. I'm ready for answers, and I'm afraid if I don't get them soon, I'll go postal on the receptionist.

Muffled voices, crying children, and groans of pain can be heard in the waiting room all around us. Every time I take a breath in through my nose, I'm taken back to the night that my brother died. It's that clinical smell, like disinfectant and metal that hangs in the air at all hospitals. My chest feels like it's in a vice as I wait impatiently to hear from the doctor and fight memories of the last time I saw Matt.

The thought of Jill finding Mindy in our house makes me sick to my stomach. I can't imagine what was going through Jill's head when she realized what was happening. I knew Mindy was unhinged; I just didn't realize how far she'd go to get me back. When I tried to get a restraining order, the police said I had to have proof that I was being stalked.

We filed a complaint after she showed up at the office on Monday, but that wasn't enough for the restraining order. I knew she was stalking us, but she was sneaky about it. Now I may have lost the love of my life because of that crazy bitch. I never should have gone to that bar and picked her up that night. I should've just manned up and fought for Jill in the first place, instead of trying to distract myself. I can't help but feel this is all my fault.

Several hours later, Cici and Denton blaze into the ER with wild eyes, holding hands. As soon as they spot me, Cici drops Denton's hand, and she's in my arms.

"I'm sorry I didn't get there sooner. I thought I heard a scream but wasn't sure until I heard it again. Denny and I grabbed our guns out of the dresser drawers and were out of there. I'm so sorry. How is she?"

"You didn't do anything wrong. Mindy's car wasn't parked at the house. I would've walked in on that crazy situation not knowing anything was wrong if it weren't for you two. Thank you. I don't know how she is. They haven't come out to find us yet, but I don't think she was breathing at the house. I couldn't tell if she had a pulse or not. I was too busy panicking."

She backs up, and Denton comes in for a

handshake half-hug that's typical for us guys. He's quiet, but concern lingers in his eyes.

He slaps my back twice and says, "Anything you need, man. If we can do it, we will."

"I know, Denton. You two are good friends. I'll let you know. What did the police say? I thought for sure you'd be there all night."

"Well, we aren't out of the woods yet. Someone will be coming by to ask you questions here soon. Internal affairs is already involved, so it will be a little dicey, but it helped that Mindy's car was found around the corner, parked at that empty lot, and that she doesn't have a permit to carry a gun. They found the report you filed earlier this week, and the officer that was questioning us let it slip that there was also a prior stalking charge against her a couple of years ago. I think it will be fine. Cici's not worried about it. Even if it's not okay, we wouldn't do anything different than we did."

The hard plastic chair under my ass is causing my back to hurt, so I twist my torso in the opposite direction of my legs hoping to crack my back. When that doesn't do the trick, I stand and walk to the sliding glass doors and step outside. The night is cool, but humid, and a storm is blowing in on the breeze. I pace back and forth for a while until Tara finally comes outside and grabs my hand. She holds it tight and stands at my side.

Her voice is soft as she says, "I really do like her. I think she's perfect for you. It's going to be okay. It has to be."

"Thanks, Tara. I love her, you know, like I've never loved anyone before. I want to marry her and raise Mariah as mine. I'll tell her the truth, that Matt was her real father once she's old enough, but I want to be her daddy. I want more kids, too. I want little league practice and dance classes and snotty noses and parent teacher conferences. I want it all, but I only want it with Jill. What if she's not okay?"

Releasing my hand, she nuzzles into my side and wraps her arms around my waist the best that she can. She doesn't say a word.

"It was bad. There was blood everywhere, and I don't think she had a pulse. I did mouth to mouth, but I was afraid I'd make it worse if I did chest compressions. I don't think I can live without her. I never thought I'd love anyone like this."

"She loves you, too, big brother. I'm glad you found that out. She'll come back to you."

Around three in the morning, a doctor strolls through the double doors looking disheveled.

"Family of Jillian Pierce?" he calls out.

We all stand and follow him to a less crowded area where he explains her injuries to us. "She's alive and the prognosis is positive, but we will know more in the next twenty-four hours."

There's an audible sigh of relief amongst our group, and I thank the doctor before he disappears down the hallway.

They are only going to let Dad and me in to see her within the hour, the doctor said. She's not conscious, and they don't want any disturbances in ICU at this time of night. The doctor explained that they are strict about visiting hours. Denton takes Cici home, and my family waits with me for the nurse to escort us to her room.

When the nurse arrives, I send Bobby and Tara home and ask Steve to wait for us in the visitor's area. I need him right now. Just having him here helps.

As soon as we enter the room and my eyes fall on her placid form, my heart cracks, and I practically crumble. My dad squeezes my shoulder and pushes me forward, so I get closer. The lighting in the room is dim, and she's covered up to her chest by a hospital blanket. The rhythmic buzz of the respirator and the constant beep of the heart monitor keep me alert. Her face is black and blue, and a jagged row of stitches runs from midway up her forehead to somewhere in her hairline. The rest of her hair is still matted with blood, and both of her eyes are rimmed with dark black and blue coloring. Angry red scratches glisten with ointment across her cheekbone and down her neck. I move the blanket enough to find her tiny hand and place my much larger one over the top of it, careful not to touch the angry red welts left behind from the rope that bound her hands. I bow my head and pray fervently for the first time in years.

After we've seen her, my dad drives home, and Steve takes me to his house. We aren't sure how long my house will be off limits since it's a crime scene. Besides I need to see Mariah. Her pack 'n' play crib is set up in the guest room, so I tip toe into the room and remove my shirt and shoes. I lean over the top and peer into the crib. She's flat on her stomach with her jammie-clad limbs splayed out like a starfish. Her sweet brown ringlets fan out around her head and over her chubby cheek. She's peaceful. I smooth the hair on her face away with delicate strokes and lean in to kiss her forehead. Then I lay down and fall asleep watching her back rise and fall with each breath, so thankful that she's not old enough to know any of this is going on and will never remember it later in life.

A couple of hours later, I'm awakened by the squawking of a happy baby by my ear. I lift one eyelid and scan the room. The second follows suit, and I see Mariah standing in the crib holding the top bar. She's smashing her face into the mesh side and yelling baby words into the air. I sit up and smile at her. She thrusts her arms in the air, falls back on her bottom, and yells "Daddadadada!"

I know she has no idea what that means. We never say daddy in conjunction with anyone, but the thought of her calling me that one day causes a grin to spread across my face as I lean forward to pull her to my chest for a cuddle. I raspberry her neck and let her pull my goatee like always. It's almost my favorite part of every day when we do this. I muddle my way to the kitchen where Mary stands cooking eggs and bacon. She eyeballs me from head to toe and gives me a sad smile.

"Go get in the shower. You have to clean up a little."

I look down to find dried blood still on parts of my arms and some on my chest and stomach.

Mary holds her hands out for Mariah and says, "Pass her here. I'll finish breakfast and change her diaper. Once you're clean, you need to come eat. Steve called the hospital and pretended to be you to find out how things are going this morning. You have an hour and a half before they'll let you in to see her again. She's stable. Not out of the woods, but stable is good.

"Your dad is going to keep Mariah for a little while so that Judy and I can come up to the hospital during visiting hours today. Your mom wore your dad out last night because she got left at home. Your dad says she's a mess and needs to see Jill for herself."

I nod my head because that sounds about right. During Mom's surgery, recovery, and treatment, she and Jill have gotten really close. I can't imagine how she feels right now.

****

Jill is in ICU for three long days before being moved to a different floor. It's been five days since the shooting, and it looks like she will make a full recovery. She'll have several scars, but at least she has her life. We're hoping to take her home in a day or two. Cici and Denton were cleared by internal affairs this morning, and we are all relieved. I wave at the nurses seated at the nurses' station as I make my way to Jill's room. When I stride through the door, I walk straight to her and kiss her lips.

"Hi, honey." I flash her a giddy smile and her right eyebrow raises in question. "Feeling okay? Did you sleep okay?"

"Yes, and yes." Her hair is a little wild from lack of brushing and styling, but Tara has her hairdresser coming in to tame it for Jill today. Before she has a chance to protest or start asking questions, I sit on the edge of the bed facing her. She raises the head of her bed a little more, and I lean in to kiss the lips I love so much one more time.

"I bought something for you this morning."

"You did? Why? I don't need anything."

"I beg to differ. This is not how I planned for this to go, but I refuse to wait another single second."

I remove the small velvet box from my pocket and

kneel next to the bed. Her eyes grow huge. It's the expression she gets every time she's about to panic, but I'm not worried this time.

"Jillian, the best day of my life was the day I met you and Mariah. You're the most beautiful woman I've ever seen and the sweetest, too. You're strong, kind, smart, and capable. I've never been more scared of losing anything in my life than I was when you were lying on that floor. I love you now, and I'll love you forever. I just want you to say yes to being my wife. I know how you operate now. You go speechless, your eyes get big like those lemur things in Madagascar, and your head spins. I know you need time to process these things, and I'll give it to you. I won't leave this room, though, until you agree to be my wife. It's inevitable. If it's today, next week, next month, or next year, it doesn't matter. It's going to happen, and you know it. So let me love you. Let me adopt Mariah. Let me be your husband, so I never again have to say the name Jillian *Pierce*. Marry me?"

I pry the little black box open with my bulky fingers, and the stone within sparkles perfectly. In that moment, I'm so thankful I had the foresight to take my sister to help pick it out. Without a word, Jill takes the ring out of the box and studies it. Her eyes lift to mine.

"This is one time I don't need to think about it. I love you, Johnny, and I want to be a Browning. More specifically I want to be *your* Browning. Yes, I'll marry you."

I jar her a little too hard when I dive for her lips, ready to seal the deal and she cries out.

"I'm sorry, baby. Are you okay?"

"Yeah, I'm better than okay. I'm getting married.

But I might have to kill you for asking me when I look like this. I'm disgusting." She huffs as she pats her hair self-consciously.

"No, you're beautiful. Now let me put my ring on your finger. I don't want any of these doctors running around here getting any ideas about asking you out.

"Dad is going to bring Mariah up to see you for a few minutes later today after you get your hair done. She's been screeching 'Mamma' while dragging herself from room to room at their house looking for you."

She sighs. "God, I miss my baby."

"I know you do, honey. She'll be here in a little while. Speaking of which, I'd better call everyone to tell them you said yes."

A few hours later my dad, Mariah, and I are visiting Jill. Keeping a toddler busy in a room full of wires, tubes, and buttons is no easy feat. Dad takes her for a walk while we talk a little longer. When the nurse comes in to help her to the bathroom, I wander off to find them. After fifteen or twenty minutes, we all return to find two very stern, irritated-looking people standing on the other side of the bed. The woman favors Jill, and my spine stiffens at the recognition. These must be her parents.

"What are you doing here?" I grind out, minus a smile.

Jill's head turns toward me, and I can tell she's been crying.

The man speaks, "I'm here to see my daughter."

"Why? Didn't you disown her and *'Satan's child'* when she was in the hospital after the car accident?"

The man stutters and stumbles over his words. "We saw her name on the news. She *is* our daughter."

I walk over and stand at her bedside and ask, "Why are you crying, honey?"

She shifts sad green eyes from the blanket bunched up in her hands to mine. She shakes her head and says, "I don't want to talk about it right now."

Her eyes flick to her parents and back to me.

"What did you say to her this time?" My voice is raised, and I'm having a hard time containing my irritation.

"Nothing she doesn't deserve," her mother haughtily answers.

"So you told her you love her and she's a wonderful person and you're so glad she's alive?" The sarcasm in my voice is thick like molasses.

"Well, no. She's living in sin. As long as she keeps living her life this way she'll keep ending up in a hospital bed or maybe even dead, roasting in the pits of hell."

"Wow. You could have stayed home and saved that speech for someone who believes it and who cares what you have to say. You will never speak to my fiancée with anything but love and care. If you can't do that, then you won't see her. She is beautiful, kind, and competent. Nothing you say to her can change that, and I won't let you hurt her in the process."

"Young man, she is an ungodly woman. We raised her better than her jezebel ways. You're leading her farther down the path of sin and estrangement from Christ," her stern-faced father aims to remind me.

From behind me my dad booms, "I don't know who you think you are, but their spiritual life is none of your business. Your judgment is not wanted or necessary. Now, unless you're here to wish her well or show some love to my granddaughter, then I expect you to get out."

"You have no right to tell us that," her father spits back, eyes bulging, face red.

My dad hoists Mariah into his arms and Mrs. Pierce's face goes white as a sheet; she must not have seen her when Dad was talking.

"I have every right in this world to protect my family. Jill is a member of my family, and I won't let you hurt her anymore. It's about time someone stood up to you. I may be old, but I can still kick your wrinkled old ass back to Indiana if you test my patience."

Mariah leans forward and nosedives for Jill. I grab her before she lands on Jill's chest. Mrs. Pierce's eyes follow her every movement.

"Is this her?" she asks in a whisper.

I don't even give Jill a chance to answer.

"This is *our* daughter, Mariah."

"Your child? I thought her father was dead," her dad questions.

"Her biological father is dead, yes, but she is my daughter. I'm adopting her. I've been helping to raise her."

By the pinched expression on Jill's dad's face, I think he's about to blow a gasket. Jill's mom has tears in her eyes as she watches Mariah crawl across the bed and try to get down.

"Here is an FYI for you folks. Unless you want a real relationship with Jillian, without judgments and hateful words, then you're no longer welcome in Jill or Mariah's presence. You people have put her through enough over the years, and she deserves to only be around people that love her and believe in her. If you plan to be supportive and loving, you are welcome back. Otherwise, I don't want to see your faces or hear that you've tried to contact her. Now if you don't leave, I will call security."

Mariah gazes up at Jill's mom from the end of the bed and smiles, and I swear that melts half the ice on her heart. She reaches out and softly strokes Mariah's cheek with one finger.

Then she grips her husband's arm and says, "Except for the eyes, she looks just like Jill when she was a baby."

Instead of looking at Mariah, he grabs his wife's hand and jerks her from the room. When they get to the hall, we can hear a verbal scuffle ensue. Although voices are raised, we can't make out anything being said. It quiets down once more, and her mother comes back into the room. She watches me warily as she approaches Jill.

"She's beautiful, Jillian, and so happy. That's really all I ever wanted for you and Isaiah. I'm not sure where I went so wrong."

She starts to leave the room and Jill speaks up, "You listened too much to my father and not enough to what the scripture really says or what you knew was right. Johnny was correct. I'll never let you or anyone else treat me like you did before. If you decide you want to try again with me, you can call me."

Jill's eyes meet mine as she requests, "Johnny, can you give my mother my phone number?"

I nod reluctantly and walk to the nurses' station to find a piece of paper and a pen to get it for her. My dad stands like a sentry by the door as Mariah toddles around the room touching everything.

Tiffani Lynn

****

Jill

Johnny has just left the room as I continue. "Mom, I'm serious. I'm open to a relationship with you and allowing Mariah to build one with you, but only if you can follow Johnny's guidelines. I love my family and will protect them at all costs."

"But Jill, *we* are your family."

"By birth only, Mother. The way you've both treated me over the years isn't a horror I'd wish on anyone. I've learned that love makes people a family, not a name. Take care of yourself, Mother." I dismiss her by turning my head away. Without another word, my mom walks out of the room pausing only to peek back at Mariah once.

Johnny returns to the room and lets me know that he gave the number to my mom but wasn't happy about it. I tell him that we will see if she even uses it before we get worked up about anything else.

Not even half an hour later, Cici shows up with Denton in tow. They have been to visit every day since the shooting, and Cici spends a crazy amount of time talking my ears off. I love her. She's funny, outgoing, and just the kind of person I need in my life. She promised to take me to the gun range and teach me how to shoot. I tease her all the time that I will get her a superhero cape because she saved my life. Apparently, after Mindy shot me, she dragged me away from the door and was poised to shoot me again when Cici fired at her through the glass in the front door. Thank goodness the circumstances surrounding the incident were clear enough to get her through an internal affairs investigation. I'm not sure how I'd feel if she lost her job because of me.

I even received flowers and a note from Mindy's parents apologizing. They mentioned that she's been on medication for years, and they weren't aware that she'd stopped taking it several months before the attack. It was obvious they felt bad, but I don't blame them. She was a grown woman and should be responsible for her own actions. The doctor prescribed sleeping medication for me, because I'm so afraid of the dreams that accompany sleep, reliving the moments I was at her mercy, I'm fighting sleep. It's been rough.

I'm taking Tara's recommendation and going to her counselor once I get out of here, which should be in a day or two. One of the nurses mentioned that I probably have PTSD, which coupled with the prior experiences of my life makes getting help a priority.

Mary has come up here about every other day since she's helping Johnny after work with Mariah, and we've had plenty of time to talk, too. It's really nice to have girlfriends for a change, people I can talk to about everything and not feel self-conscious. Cici has convinced Mary and me to join her and her other friends for girls' night out when I'm healed. Life is good right now, even if I'm recovering from a gunshot wound. For the first time in my life, I'm content, happy even with my relationships and a future I can finally see with more clarity than ever before.

Epilogue

Jill
Two months later

I'm in the back room of a beautiful little country church. Today we're getting married. Mariah is outside right now with Cici's mom, running her ragged, I'm sure. Cici just finished with my hair, and Mary is holding up my dress for me to step into. Valerie is standing off to the side with the camera and a sweet smile on her face. Judy is on the other side with tears in her eyes and a camera in her hand, waiting for me to be covered up before she starts snapping pictures.

My dress is an off-white, strapless, column sheath with intricate beading all over the bodice. I had planned to find a simple white summer dress to wear, but Johnny insisted that I get an actual dress and we have an actual wedding. His exact comment was, "Hon, we are not going to the justice of the peace to get married. We're having a real wedding in a real church, and then we're having a real reception to celebrate it. When that's done, we're having a real honeymoon. We're only getting married once in our lives, so we are doing it right."

I confessed to him later that night I was sad that I wouldn't have anyone on my side of the church, an embarrassment for me. That's when he told me there is no bride and groom's side at our wedding, and the ushers would seat everyone evenly down both sides. Since our family is the same, there is no need to separate them. I couldn't argue with that, so I didn't.

Cici and Mary helped me throw together a wedding in record time. Judy is done with chemo and radiation, and although it was a difficult road for her, she's been given the all-clear. She's in remission.

Johnny won't tell me where we are going for the honeymoon, only that he's taking care of it. Mary, Steve, Judy, and John are taking turns watching Mariah while we are away, so everything is taken care of. Now, I just have to step into my four-inch high heels and walk down the aisle toward my soon-to-be husband.

The double doors leading into the sanctuary are opened by our ushers, Denton and Eduardo. I have John on my left side. He's giving me away since my father and I still aren't on speaking terms. On my right, holding my hand is an antsy Mariah in a light pink, chiffon flower girl dress. She had a cute flowered headband on, but being a year old, she decided she didn't want that so it's currently in Judy's purse, and her little brown ringlets are wild on her head. Johnny insisted that she join us for the vows since he's getting both of us with this ceremony. Johnny filed the paperwork to adopt her last week. The plan is for her to walk down the aisle with John and me, so we will see if that fits with her toddler agenda once we get in the sanctuary.

Right as the music starts, I hear the door from the outside behind me close, and I glance back to find my mother standing there. Her hand is covering her mouth as she stares at me, and her eyes glisten with tears. She's in a homely floral dress and has her hair in the same severe bun that she's worn all of my life. I'm shocked to see her, but I try not to let that show.

Before I can say anything, Mariah breaks loose from me and runs to my mom, crashing into her legs and grabbing hold. That kid is too friendly for her own good. This will be the first time she's seen my mom since the hospital room. I've only talked to her twice and both times, I hung up not sure what to think. I didn't realize she was coming today; she never RSVP'd one way or the other.

The bridal march music is playing, and everyone is standing inside waiting for me, but I'm rooted to the spot watching this unfold in front of me. John speaks up and calls Mariah to him. She runs straight to his arms, and he picks her up. Then he turns to my mom and says, "I'm glad you could make it. Go on in ahead of us and have a seat. You can see the girls after the ceremony."

My mom nods and walks up next to me.

She leans in and kisses my cheek and whispers, "You really are beautiful."

Then she turns the corner and finds a spot to sit a few pews up. John hands Mariah to me. I put her down on my right side again and grab her tiny hand so we can make our way down the aisle.

Halfway down, Mariah breaks free of my grip and does a toddler sprint to Johnny who scoops her right up and nuzzles her neck. By the time I'm standing in front of them, she's pulling on his goatee and smacking his face, the same thing she's done since the day he met her. He's smiling with tears in his eyes as the preacher asks, "Who gives this woman in marriage?"

John answers, "My wife and I do." The pride in his

voice causes my lip to quiver a little as he places my hand in Johnny's. With a chaste kiss to my cheek, he steps away and takes his seat next to Judy.

We wrote our own vows. Mine are good, but Johnny's take the cake. He addresses his vows to both Mariah and me, and promises to love and cherish us both always. The whole time we are reciting them, Mariah is perched on his hip between us. One minute she's pulling his goatee and the next she's plucking at the beading on my dress. I'm sure some people think it's tacky, but to me it means the world.

At the reception, I notice my mother dancing with Mariah and I almost fall over. She has always been against dancing of any kind, but apparently, all it took was a toddling grandchild to change her mind about that. It's the first time I've seen my mother smile since I got the Bible Verse Reciting Award in second grade. I'm happy, but also afraid to hope that things will be different with her now.

****

It turns out that Johnny booked us at an all-inclusive adult-only beachside resort in Jamaica. The place is amazing, but we don't spend much time enjoying the sights, instead we stay naked and tangled in each other the entire time. It's the most romantic, relaxing week of my life, and I have a feeling that with Johnny's determination we should see the fruits of our labor this week in about nine months' time.

****

Johnny
One year later

We were already running late because she had to finish a paper she's been working on for two weeks.

I'm so glad that she chose to go back to college to finish her degree, even if she stays working with me forever. I feel like she deserves to file a bachelor's degree as another accomplishment in her self-worth folder. She needs to realize that she can do whatever she sets her mind to. I'm really proud of the hard work she's put in, but now I have to get her butt moving.

"Mariah and Melissa are strapped in. Get a move on, or we'll have two screaming kids for the car ride. I'm not sure I can deal with that again," I yell to my wife as I lean in through the door from the garage to the house.

"I had to change shirts. Melissa spit up all over me, and I was not going to see my brand new nephew covered in puke," she yells back to me.

"Jesse is a newborn. He doesn't care what the hell you're wearing. He *will* care if his cousins are screaming banshees, now come on."

I go back to the garage and get in the car. I'm only waiting for about thirty seconds before my wife hustles through the door, hair flying behind her, a scowl on her face.

"I hate being rushed," she complains.

"I know, honey. I just want to be able to enjoy this day without screaming kids to start it." I smile at her, hoping to disarm her. "You are beautiful."

Her scowl slips away and she leans over to kiss me.

"Thanks, baby. Let's go to Steve and Mary's. I can't wait to get my hands on their little boy."

****

Later that night, once both girls are in bed and we are curled around each other quietly exploring with our hands and fingers, she whispers, "I love our life,

Johnny."

"Me, too, honey."

I lean up on an elbow and slide my hand up to cup her plump breast. Each is larger than I've ever seen because she's breastfeeding Melissa, and it's so damn sexy I can't stand it. She says she feels like a milk cow and not a sexy wife, but I tell her she's wrong and go about worshiping her curvier body, licking her nipples lightly before moving south on her. Me sucking on them at this stage freaks her out, so I settle for using my mouth at the juncture of her thighs instead. It seems after having our baby that her body is more sensitive all over. Just breathing on her sex has her arching and moaning for me. I part her lips with my fingers and slowly lap at her inner folds, never quite hitting her sensitive bundle of nerves. The begging starts. I live for the begging. It's the reason I haven't made direct contact yet.

"Please, Johnny. Please, Johnny. Don't make me wait tonight. I need it." She continues to beg, so I give in and suck on her clit hard, working it with my tongue as I do. I haven't made it a whole minute, and she's falling apart underneath me. When I'm certain she's wrung dry, I pull my body up even with hers, nudge her legs farther apart with my knees, and enter her as slowly as I can.

Her eyes flutter open and make contact with mine. I roll my hips into her as I stay back on my heels ready to watch the action from this vantage point. She breaks eye contact first and hoists herself onto her elbows so she can watch, too.

Her eyes flare when I withdraw and push back in again. "Harder, baby. You know I like it harder."

227

I smile at her and comply, adjusting myself so my arms are on either side of her, giving me the leverage to power into her. I lower my face into her neck and inhale her natural scent that seems laced with baby lotion these days. I lick my way up her neck and suck on the tender spot behind her ear. Goose bumps spread across her skin and her legs lock tighter around my hips.

"I love you, baby," she tells me in a soft, sweet voice and that ends my control. Unglued, I pump into her hard until I feel her tighten around my cock and a strangled sound rolls out of her mouth. Her limbs stay locked around me, but her rigid muscles have gone limp, so I power into her for a few more strokes before I erupt inside her.

"Keep that up, baby and you're going to knock me up again," she says on a giggle.

"You're on the pill. That won't happen, but if it did, that would be okay by me. You're fucking hot pregnant."

She playfully smacks my arm and says, "I looked like a house pregnant. It was not attractive."

"Yeah, it was. I loved nothing more than to see your naked, round belly sticking out from our sheets in the morning. I've never seen anything more amazing than your body change as you carried her. I love you, Jilli. Don't ever forget that, with a baby or without a baby. There's never been a more beautiful woman or two more lovely girls than mine."

About the Author

Tiffani was born in Texas but has lived all over the United States. She currently resides in Florida with her husband, three daughters, and her dog. She graduated from the University of Maryland with a degree in social science and spent five years working for Hospice. When she's not writing or taxiing her children around, she enjoys reading and attending concerts. Tiffani is also a crazed fan of the Tampa Bay Lightning, Tampa Bay Rays, and the 2016 World Series Champion Chicago Cubs.

~*~

Visit Tiffani at
www.tiffanilynn.com

~*~

To chat with Tiffani Lynn and other Wild Rose Press authors of erotic romance, join us at
www.groups.yahoo.com/group/thewilderroses.

Also Available

Strangers at Sunset
Betrayal to Bliss Book One
by Tiffani Lynn

https://amzn.com/B01IFQT2AO

When newly widowed Lisa Browning discovers her late-husband has fathered a child with another woman, she abandons that vat of ice cream with her name on it and flies off to Florida for a job interview with hopes of a new life. Lured by the sunset and lulled by the sound of the waves, she becomes the focus of a sexy photographer on and off camera. He's the perfect substitute for her vat of ice cream…until her heart gets in the way.

Freelance photographer Garrett Kline is looking for the perfect subject for his latest job. When he spots the sensual siren on the beach, he's found what he is looking for…and then some. His inner playboy is good with a short-term fling, but something about Lisa makes him want more than being just strangers at sunset.

Also Read

Deep Down
Kings of California Book One
by Mia Hopkins

https://amzn.com/B016ZGXS4M

Sex, drugs, and spicy tuna rolls?
Resilient and disciplined, tsunami survivor Eve Ono moves to California from Japan looking for a position as a sushi chef. When she's suddenly fired from her restaurant job, desperation drives her to find work on a fishing boat despite her fears of the ocean. To make matters worse, she's stuck in close quarters with her new captain—a man whose raw physicality drives her out of her mind with lust.

Free-spirited and roguish, Sam Lamont is a commercial fisherman aboard his own dive boat, the Bravado. When he makes a bad deal with a deadly loan shark who threatens to take his boat, Sam is in danger of losing both his business and his way of life. On top of that, he's got to train his new deckhand—a beautiful hard-ass who just so happens to be sexy as hell.

A female sushi chef with mad knife skills. A deep-sea diver who's pissed off a Mexican drug cartel. Together, they're in trouble, and the only way out is down.

Thank you for purchasing this
publication of The Wild Rose Press, Inc.
If you enjoyed the story, we would appreciate
your letting others know by leaving a review.
For other wonderful stories, please visit our
on-line bookstore at www.wilderroses.com.

For questions or more
information contact us at
info@thewildrosepress.com.

The Wild Rose Press, Inc.
www.thewilderroses.com

Stay current with The Wild Rose Press, Inc.
Like us on Facebook
https://www.facebook.com/TheWildRosePress
And Follow us on Twitter
https://twitter.com/WildRosePress

www.ingramcontent.com/pod-product-compliance
Lightning Source LLC
Chambersburg PA
CBHW070924180626
46817CB00003B/1183